WE GO BUMP

Creepypasta
Wiki
Anthology

VOLUME 1

Edited and Assembled by: Andrew Movitz

DEDICATION

This book is for all of our writers on the Creepypasta Wiki. The good, the bad, the poor, the new, the seasoned, the weird. Keep writing. Keep trying. They can't all be winners, but at least one might be. Try. Try some more. If you think you might give up, stop and take a break. Then, try later.

CONTENTS

ACKNOWLEDGMENTS

A big thank you to all the admin and mods on the Creepypasta Wiki for keeping the site safe and (mostly) sane, and a huge thanks to everyone who participated in this book. Thank you to everyone who submitted stories and to everyone who spent their precious time hammering them out. All stories included with authors' permission; all rights reserved. All content is presented as-is, with minor editing to keep the author's vision intact.

41488p

"Hi there. I'm a set of numbers and a letter. Also, I'm one digit from the error. I've been writing for a year or two, since I discovered that "talent" a year ago. I wouldn't call my writing the best out there, but recently I've been doing some horror writing, since I just can't resist writing about things that could creep people out. Making readers think is one thing. Making them turn around at every small sound is another, more skillful thing. In this anthology, I have submitted two of my "best" works, and by "best", I mean it has a plot that would actually creep someone out, and the writing's decent enough. I hope you enjoy reading them and the other pastas, and I hope you enjoy your night. Thanks."

High

By: 41488p

"So, basically, I asked Jen out... guess what she said?"

My friend rolled his eyes. "We were all high that night, Jason. Yes?"

"Hell, YES!" to quote her exact words. Does it matter, though? We're in a relationship now, Aaron, a freakin' relationship!" I twisted the laptop around to prove my point.

Aaron stared at it. "Tell me you didn't just update your relationship status on Facebook."

"Heck yeah I did."

Aaron sighed. "Listen, Jason, she's already dating someone."

I was rendered speechless for ten seconds straight.

"No way."

"Yes way, Jason. Look, everyone was high that night. You seriously expect to believe a high person in a party?"

"Well, at least it's a start. Hey, did I tell you about the stuff I saw that night?"

"Shit?"

An old man sitting across from us looked up to greet the waiter that brought his meal. His eyes then shifted to us. Looking back at his food, he mumbled the stuff an old guy would mumble to 'those college guys', then promptly picked up his fork, and stabbed the steak.

"Jason?"

I shifted my attention back to Aaron. "You want to hear the story?"

"Sure."

"So, basically, when we were alone in the dining room, cleaning up after everyone got knocked out, I heard some scratching from the front door. Then a pair of red eyes staring through the window. Then a triple rainbow. Just kidding."

I saw Aaron's shoulders, which had been hunched up before, loosen up a little. I went on.

"But, the eyes? Personal experience, man," I thumped my chest, studying the forehead of Aaron, which was glistening with sweat all of a sudden. "Personal experience. Nice story, huh?"

Aaron looked scared. He usually wasn't scared. I looked behind him again, at the old man. He was almost done gobbling up his steak.

"Jason?" Aaron stammered.

" 'Scuse me?"

"Did you take lots of crack?"

"Well, not reall-"

"I don't think you were high, man."

"What are you saying?"

As Aaron went on his rant about the hallucinations of crack, my vision just seemed to float back to the old man. He waved for the bill, his red eyes glistening under the chandelier that was hanging above him. After he paid the bill, he got up and left.

"Jason, I'm scared."

Aaron was shaking real bad. My vision rested back to Aaron, but not until noticing the peculiarly sharp fingernails of the old man.

Loot

And for the 14th and last time, the mansion's doors were broken open. The thief stood there, panting, a fire axe in his hands. He had originally planned to make this mansion his home for the time being, since it was easy to defend against the walking dead, but as he comprehended the scene in front of him (which consisted now of a few broken panes of glass and some wood which could now only be used as firewood), he was rethinking his plan.

"Nah," he said to himself. "Just loot and go. Take some food. Supplies."

It turned out to be more difficult that he imagined it would be to loot this monster of a house. Its previous inhabitants, having fled the house years ago, when the first of the dead rose, apparently took nothing.

The thief stroked his hands across dozens of gold necklaces and earrings. He looked around again, and admired himself in the titanic mirror the room boasted. And this was just one of the many rooms occupying this mansion.

"Sexy," he whispered, cuddling a gold pendant he hung around his neck.

He looked outside the window. It was getting dark. And there were more rooms to loot.

He made his way carefully across the old, rotting house. The floorboards could give way any minute, and with all the loot he stuffed inside his backpack (which he planned to sell tonight at the safehouse for some; no, a lot of supplies), he didn't want to die now.

"Would we?" he half-thought, half-spoke as the zombie strutted out of a room in front of him. He quietly took out his axe and readied it for a swing.

"See you in hell fuckah!" he shouted as the tip of his axe made contact with the zombie's neck. It didn't even have time to cry out, and its body crashed through the railing and followed its head on the way down to the basement-

Wait. Basement.

"More sweet loot, man, more sweet loot!" he whispered. The basement would have a fortune inside of it. And gaining access to it was a trivial feat.

He walked down the stairs, his heart pounding for the first time in years not from fear, but rather from excitement.

"Three!"

He elbowed the glass out of the way and poked his head through the recently broken-down door to the basement.

Dark. Need some light.

He threw a flare down and saw that there were steps leading down.

He got out his flashlight and descended into the reddish-darkness of the basement.

It was cool inside, although it was kind of scary being in the middle of all this stuff in the dark.

He ran his hands across books, toys, everything one could imagine for in the zombie apocalypse.

And then he spotted it.

He literally ran for the cardboard box sitting on the shelves. With his flashlight in his mouth, he tore the box open and watched in amazement as dozens of packets of potato chips fell onto the dusty floor.

He looked behind him, took out his axe, and flung it at the box he was looking at.

He was immediately drenched in fresh water. He reached into the broken box and took out an intact water bottle, opening it while salivating like a rabid dog.

He cried out in joy as the fresh water poured down his throat.

"Psst, man, over here."

He dug his mind out of the comic book and searched for the source of the noise.

"Yeah, man, I know it's dark, but with my current situation and all, y'know, I can't really turn on the lights."

The thief got up.

"Wh-who's there?"

"Can't you see? Hear me? Like a fuckin' bat?"

The voice was coming from the right. The thief turned on his flashlight.

"Yayaya yada yada ya. CAN'T YOU HEAR ME NOW YOU IMBECILE?"

The thief checked to see if he was dreaming. Pinch. Pinch. Still awake.

"Deaf mute fucker. Can't even hear."

"You..." The thief blinked his eyes.

The voice was coming from a box.

"Yeah, yeah, tear me open like you did with the Lays, but don't do it like with the whassa-that-brand water thing. Yeah, yeah. I can feel the light, man! I can FEEEL it!"

The thief, mouth sore from holding a large flashlight in it for so long, finally gave up.

"Look, whoever you are, I can't..." He panted. "The tape's...tape's too...thick..."

"Balls. You don't have them. The box next to me is filled with soccer balls."

The thief looked desperately at the boxes around him. It was probably close to night outside already, and he lost his knife by throwing it at a mob of the walking dead earlier today.

"Knives. Thassait. Look at the box below me."

The thief knocked the talking box to the ground (which elicited a very pissed-off response from the box) and opened the box below it with ease, finding that the talking box wasn't lying.

"Youssa got it? Ow. My ass. Oh wait. I don't have one." Maniac's laughter.

"Yeah, I've got it."

The thief gripped the knife, stabber-style, and proceeded to cut open the box, wondering all the time why it was covered in so many layers of tape.

Finally, he got it.

The last layer of tape came off, and the thief was faced with the contents of the box.

"Hey. You're bad-lookin'," the mask in the box said.

The thief looked at the mask in disbelief. Finally, he got his mouth to say something: "You're a mask."

"Yeah, and we're surrounded by zombies and shit. Whaddya know? It's a fucked up world. Welcome to it." The mask frowned (can masks change expressions?). "You seem older than four. Oh. Fucked up world. Maybe you are four."

The thief picked up the mask. "Who-what are you?"

"Put me on, yeah, put me on and we'll go flying away."

The thief hesitated. "Why would I do that? I've seen enough today alread-"

"Oh, when you put me on, it's like a never-ending orgasm. You're gonna be the richest man in the world. Best shot in the county. Heck, the universe. You put me on, you never regret it. You won't look back." The mask winked. "Nobody does." It paused, seemingly thinking. "Oh yeah, I'm also the sweetest loot in the entire house."

"Sweetest loot..." The thief, in a daze, put the mask on.

The dead outside the house heard maniacal laughter from the basement.

And for the first and last time, the thief went to his safehouse with a purpose other than to sell loot.

Azure-Clarity

"Greetings, darlings~ My name is Claire and I am simply a multifaceted artist. And a hippie. Though my appearance is bright and eccentric, I love to delve deeply into imaginary worlds not even the beasts of your nightmares dare venture near. That is, when I'm not busy feeding the squirrels. There is an idea of me, some kind of ludicrous nonsense that involves physically assaulting idiots with my otherwise useless degree in creative writing, but there is no real me. Only an entity. Something illusory. And though I can hide my piercings, and you can shake my hand and feel my manicured nails digging into your flesh, and maybe you can even sense that my lifestyle is psychotic compared to yours, I simply am not there."

Welcome Home

By: Azure-Clarity

I grew up in a small Midwestern town where the whole community was tight-knit. Our families didn't just consist of our parents, but everyone else, too. The neighborhood kids were siblings by a different name. People rarely strayed and even more seldom did strangers move in, but they were welcomed as if they had always belonged there.

The last outsider to ever settle in the town was a woman named Maria Sigrid. She was a beautiful young woman, looking no older than late twenties. Despite having no children of her own, she had a loving maternal aura that naturally drew us kids towards her. I think part of it was her eyes. They were chestnut, but the life and the kindness they glimmered with gave them the mesmerizing countenance of being golden.

She bought the little two-story building that stood empty for as long as anyone could remember. I'd seen that place only once shortly before Maria's arrival. It still serves to be the oldest memory I can recollect. It was decrepit, almost falling to pieces at its very foundation. Its yellowing paint was chipped and weathered by years of neglect, but a lot of that was hidden by the ivy and other types of flora that had begun to overwhelm the decaying corpse of a home.

The next time I saw that building, it had undergone a complete transmutation. Someone had clearly taken the time to invest in a much needed makeover of the place. Most of the plants that were trying to swallow the building were removed, save for a few ribbons of ivy that decorated the left-hand side.

The outside was painted a fresh red-brown color that shown to be an extreme improvement from the previous yellow-white exterior and bright pink shutters were installed on the windows. It was, for once, hospitable.

Maria had taken ownership of the place and converted the first floor into a bakery and restaurant which she called Welcome Home. The lively atmosphere and Maria's tender disposition towards visitors and customers made the moniker appropriate. It felt like a second home to everyone who stopped by and she soon became as much a mother to us kids as our own mothers. As you would expect, it didn't take long for Welcome Home to become our after-school hangout.

Since the place was small and was never completely packed with customers, Maria could alternate between attending to us and serving her clientele. She would always give us a snack from the bakery section, usually an apple pie or a chocolate cake, and we would tell her all about the exciting gossip going around the playground and what we learned that day as she listened and smiled with interest.

When the restaurant would close for the day, Maria gave us her undivided attention. She would play tons of different games with us, tell us stories that had us captivated with their vividness, and she had a special box set aside for us full of crafting supplies that we could use. Sometimes when we were too contented with whatever we were engaged in, she would observe us quietly from off to the side as she worked on her knitting, or she might wander off to make us more treats.

Halloween at Welcome Home was the best. The place would be decorated with paper ghosts, cats, witches, and pumpkins that we and Maria crafted together and outside, there would be a big Jack-o-lantern that we had all helped her to carve. It was an annual affair after trick-or-treating that we would gather in the upstairs living quarters and congregate on the floor, munching on Maria's renowned candy apples and swapping unwanted candy as she set the atmosphere with dimmed lights and candles. She would at last sit in the plush chair we all huddled around and began telling us scary stories long into the night. She never once told the same story twice, though a lot of them involved witches and children unfortunate enough to cross paths with them. They were her favorites, she explained.

By the time I was entering junior high, I was still frequenting Welcome Home as often as I always had. Everything was ordinary and there were no unusual happenings to foreshadow what was about to transpire on July 18th, 1983.

It was oddly chilly that day and overcast with heavy, grey clouds, resembling a late-September evening more so than a blistering July morning. Mrs. Packer, our neighbor who worked at the local library, could be heard screaming frantically from outside, "They're gone! They're gone!"

Everything was so chaotic those first few hours. No one knew what was going on. It wasn't until the afternoon did the sheriff come knocking on everyone's doors to explain the situation and try to get some information.

Almost half of the town's children were gone. Their beds were empty, but there was no indication that someone had forced their way into their rooms and taken them. Their bikes were still where they'd left them, so they couldn't have gone too far, yet a thorough search of the area turned up nothing.

The children weren't the only ones missing.

Maria was gone, too.

It was obvious Maria had taken the children. At first, many refused to acknowledge that. Her sweet and respectable conduct made it hard to believe that she could have kidnapped those children. Because of this, some speculated that someone else had come by in the night and kidnapped both her and the kids, but much like with the children, there was no evidence at Welcome Home that backed up that theory.

I rode my bike past Welcome Home that day the reports on the missing children came in, when the sky was turning a rusted orange. I was a skeptic, too, and I felt like somehow, looking at Maria's house would give me the answers to the questions I didn't realize I was asking.

I had to stop when I finally got there. The place looked exactly as it had before Maria took it up as her refuge. The bright pink shutters were gone. The paint job had reverted back to its chipped, decaying shade of yellowed enamel. Vegetation had once again ensnared the broken-down home like an insect caught in a Venus flytrap, completely covering the spot where the eloquently-painted sign for the restaurant and bakery used to be. It looked so bizarre and wrong to see the life Maria had put into the place sucked right out of it, like I was staring at the victim of a murder metaphorically committed.

The community grew colder in the aftermath. Not to each other, but to outsiders. New blood was rarely, if ever, welcomed. The incident had violated us of our sense of trust and security with the outside world and as a result, the ambiance of the whole town felt more closed-off and depressive. I moved away as soon as I could to separate myself from the gloom. I went to an out-of-state school and eventually found a job as a photographer.

A few years ago, my job required me to head off to this small town I never heard of that rested in the heart of Missouri to snap some photos of their historical museum. I was just heading back to my hotel after a full day of semi-nostalgic sightseeing and photography when I saw it. It was a different building, but it had the same auburn-colored paint and those pink shutters. I thought for a second I'd gone crazy, especially when I saw the sign sitting above the entryway.

Welcome Home.

I had to see for myself if this was real. I went into the building, but not before snapping a few quick pictures of the exterior and the sign.

The place was devoid of customers, but there was a woman sweeping up the floor, her russet locks spilling down her back as she hummed a tune I could almost recognize. She didn't need to turn around and show me her face. She didn't need to say anything. Just by the strong impression she left me with, I knew in an instant it was her.

"Maria," I said.

Her broom paused in mid-sweep and she turned to me with that motherly smile I had been so familiar with in my youth. Nothing about her had changed despite the thirty year lull, making her now appear younger than me. Even her eyes still held that golden luminance to them that I remembered so keenly.

"Billy," she said in recognition and I could hear her smile wafting into her tone. "I didn't think I would ever see you again. Please, take a seat." She motioned to the countertop lined with stools and I sat at the nearest one, watching as she disappeared into the kitchen.

Maria came back soon after with a steaming pot pie and placed it in front of me along with a fork. Somehow, I felt faintly hesitant to eat it, but one glance at her expectant smile gave me the incentive to start eating.

"You've gotten so big," she mused after a while. "I can still remember when you were barely up to my hip." She sighed softly, but heavy with what sounded like wistfulness.

I could have sat there and ate until I was licking the pie tin clean, but I wasn't there just for food. I had to speak with Maria. I had to ask her about that night and the children. The pie was so good, though, that I admit I had to stop myself from eating anymore so I could talk.

"Maria…" I couldn't find the nerve to ask her. As important as the issue was, no one normally comes up to someone they haven't seen in decades and asks them right off the bat if they kidnapped a handful of children.

She seemed to get what I was hinting at. Maria smiled and bowed her head as if she were contemplating how to respond. Finally, she said to me, "Once upon a time, there was a woman."

I don't generally tolerate people beating around the bush, but I remained quiet and listened to her with the same captivation I would have as a child.

"This woman was very sweet," she continued. "She was kind to everyone, especially children. This woman worked in the food industry and took great pride in it. As I'm sure you could guess, because of her pride, she would go to great lengths to make sure everything she made had the best ingredients and was prepared with the utmost care. She traveled a lot to ensure she could find a wide array of ingredients, staying in some places longer than others, but always moving on eventually."

A chuckle rose from her, after which she continued. "What no one knew about this woman was that she was a witch and the reason why the witch moved so often is because she would spirit away the town's children. She would enchant them and take them somewhere else to put them to better use. She would never take all the children, though. She wasn't that cruel."

By then, my stomach felt like it had descended past my knees. Maybe I shouldn't have raised the question, but I did. I had to. "…What would she do with the children?"

Her smile grew to a depth I'd never seen on her before, both saccharine and calculating. "The children she had taken from the town before would become prime ingredients once she set up shop in the next location and she would paint it with their blood."

My stomach churned so violently that I thought I would vomit all over the countertop. I ran out to my car and I heaved numerous times, but nothing ever came. Once I was done, I looked up and saw Maria standing in the doorway of Welcome Home, watching me with concern as if she hadn't expected this revelation to elicit such a reaction out of me.

I couldn't bare to stay any longer after that. I probably broke at least eight traffic laws on the way back to the hotel. I had trouble sleeping that night and when I did manage to catch an hour or so of rest, I had graphic nightmares of a witch slaughtering children and serving them to people who were unaware that they were cannibalizing someone else's children.

I went back there the next day. I was only able to recognize it because the structure of the building was the same as the one in the photos. It, much like the old Welcome Home in my hometown, now stood as a shell of what it once was; a rotting edifice with a chipped, blue visage and eye-like windows broken where the soul Maria had given the place was stolen.

I left the town immediately after that. On my way out, I passed a few houses where distraught parents were sobbing to police officers; something about being unable to find their children.

I still have those photos. I keep them tucked away in a box buried in my closet like a dirty secret. For the sake of my own children, I hope I never see her again…

But yesterday, my wife told me that a sweet young lady moved into the old Barrows place. Very pretty eyes, she told me. Almost golden.

C0balt Crusade

"Hi, I'm Henry, better known by my online name (for almost everything) as C0balt Crusade. I try to write actual stories, but my writing feels clunky, so I end up writing poems. I am into art, mostly drawing and painting, and also The Internet. And cats. God I love cats.

A Little Gallows Humor ~~~~~~~~~~~~~~~~~~~ **Page 20**

A Little Gallows Humor

By: C0balt Crusade

As I stand here on the hangman,

I cannot help but smirk,

For I am the one to die, then,

But your souls are spotted and dark.

I stole to feed my family,

A loaf of bread, that's all,

But if everyone could see your souls,

They would be truly appalled.

For with the bad eyesight and foresight I own,

Hindsight is where I excel,

And if my truths are told,

I'll see you all in hell.

You there! Constable Shirkin!

You say you have ne'er sinned,

But you beat your wife and child savagely,

And they have to bear and grin!

And you! Deputy Howe!

Your heart for a woman was great,

But when she loved another,

You cried "Witch!" and she was burned at the stake.

And lets not forget Sheriff Calder,

Who when his daughter was with child,

She was beaten viciously,

And her and the baby died.

So my truths have been told,

Final words with lessened tact,

And now my speech is done,

I hope you burn in-CRACK!

ChaoZStrider

"I am ChaoZStrider, I am a lover of fine foods, horror movies and games. I have a generally low expectation for myself and others around me. It does not require much to get me thinking and creating, I write and create stories in my spare time. I edit pictures that capture my interest. Most of the things I write and draw often go unposted and stored somewhere to remain hidden until I want other people see it. I listen to all kinds of music while I do many things. You see, when it comes to my stories and the stories I read, I believe the story gives a view into not only the mind of the character, but the mind of the author as well. The best stories often have the author relating to one of the characters whether it be a main character or a background character. The authors you read about and the stories you read written by them are treasures in their own way, each one being brilliant in it's own manner. Enjoy what you read and try to relate to get the best out of each story"

Haunted by My Shadow ~~~~~~~~~~~~~~~~~~~~ **Page 23**

Haunted by My Shadow

By: ChaoZStrider

I stirred as a soft breeze played across my face, I slowly opened my eyes, feeling sick and decrepit. As my eyes opened, I couldn't help but notice I was not at home, there was no roof over my head but a black blanket of space and stars visible through the leaves. I slowly made my way to an upright position, feeling sore all over, like I had just belly-flopped my way out of a bull race.

Feeling uneasy and disoriented, I started following the path of dilapidated moonlight shining on the lush forest floor. I started staggering toward the building, almost tripping a few times. Eventually I just needed to sit down again, I came across a puddle, and sat down next to it, splashing some on my face. After a few moments rest, I stood up again, but a movement in the corner of my eyes brought my gaze to the puddle, barely in the reflection of the puddle stood what appeared to be a woman with pale skin, however I couldn't see above her neck and past her belly button.

As soon as I caught sight of that ghastly image, I ran away as fast as my legs would carry me, I almost stumbled several times, but when I thought I lost her, I allowed myself to slumped down by a nearby tree. As I caught my breath, I peeked above the bushes and brambles littering the ground, I noticed two things. One, I couldn't see that women, and two, I had lost sight of that building. I cursed and sank back against the tree, trying to plan what to do next.

I figured that building may have a phone I could use to call someone or perhaps a map so I could figure out where I am, but I had to get there without that woman finding me. I considered backtracking to where I woke up, but what if that woman was still there, in my weakened state, I doubted I would fare well in a fight. I decided to stay here for a bit longer, maybe she would move on, it would also give me a chance to recuperate. I began taking deep, quiet breaths as I ran my hands through my thick dirty blonde hair and began to listen to the surrounding forest.

After listening intently for a few minutes, I heard nothing but the sounds of a gently breeze blowing the leaves around. I risked another peek, all clear.There was no sign that girl had even pursued me, the only thing that seemed to even be in this forest besides trees and that house was myself. I was sure the girl was not near, but still had the sensation of being watched, I brushed this off and slinked silently over to where I think I had started.

I couldn't help but looking over my shoulder every few moments, though every time was the same, there was nothing there. I felt like I was being mocked for not being able to see what made it feel like I was being stared at. After what felt like forever, I managed to find the spot where I originally woke up, this time I decided to take the scenic route around the puddle, determined to make it to the building. I finally reached the façade of the deteriorating building.

I swallowed my fear and walked closer, trying to comprehend the enormous felling of doom that was arising in me. As I made my way to the front of the building, I tried to glance through the windows but I soon noticed I couldn't see through them without jumping. I decided against that quickly as I did not want to make more noise than needed in case the girl was close by.

When I finally reached the front door, I twisted the door knob but to no avail, it wouldn't move. I pushed on the door a couple of times, listening carefully it seemed as if the hinges were rusted to the point the door would just fall off when pushed with enough force.

I stepped back to examine the house closer. There were vines growing everywhere, even poking through some of the broken windows. The stone was either broken or gone it seemed, and there was not a grimy window that wasn't severely broken. The door was indented in several places, and one of the hinges was hanging off, I was gonna have to muscle in.

Despite how the outside appeared, the inside was almost regal. Polished hard wood floors, the paint on the walls looked like it was painted only yesterday, crystal chandelier, beautiful white carpeted stairs, yet the feeling of being watched only got stronger. I gazed around, it felt like the darkness was pressing in on me, stunting my breathing.

The momentary effect still lingered, but the thought of continuing on petrified me. I knew going back out into the forest was not an option because of that girl, but the sound of me hitting the floor, and the door shattering would certainly draw her attention. Despite the darkness, I had to continue on before she came to check out the sound.

As I walked up the stairs, the pressure causing me to break into a cold sweat, I looked around, and saw a being to the left. I was about to scream, until I saw it was not the women, as I slowly calmed down, I looked closer. It was a mirror. I gave my reflection a quick look, I was covered in mud, and had small scratches from running through the trees, and the area I hit the door was starting to bleed through my sweater. Then I saw something that made my blood run cold, my right eye had taken a pale yellow shape, and my left eye, a minty green. I stared right into those eyes, trying not to panic. The girl with the pale skin appeared in my reflection, with the same damn eyes. I screamed just before the mirror shattered, footsteps echoing from the entrance of the house.

As I watched him stare into the mirror, I couldn't help but smile, Alex was so dirty and bloody. He looked like he had no clue of the events that had transpired just hours before waking up in that bloody forest. I decided to show the confused little Alex what I looked like before getting rid of the fucking mirror, the look on his face was priceless, so frightened and scared. The crimson liquid staining his sweater seemed to spread more as the scare increased his pulse. The sound of the footsteps coming closer was just a bonus from a little hallucination caused by being frightened.

As I ran, I felt like if I had to spend one more second in this nightmare I would go insane, get rid of this psychological torture. I just couldn't shake the feeling that there was special in this building. Something that would make life normal again. I fought back tears as I thought of my loved ones back home, what could be happening to them?

I decided it was time to reveal to Alex what was so special about this house. I began to close doors that were close to him while only leaving one door open, behind that open door was the dead body, mutilated to the point no one would be able to tell who it is. I left a little gift for Alex in that room, his watch, just ticking away on the wrist of the dead man. I couldn't help but giggle in anticipation for when Alex noticed the room, waiting to see how scared he would be.

I reached a hallway, peeling wallpaper, creaky boards, and the strong smell of decay, I heard a badly stifled giggle, and decided to not linger. I started trying doors, they wouldn't budge. After my seventh try I found an unlocked door, a puff of dust assaulted my eyes and nose as soon I opened the door, and I felt somebody tackle me. Thinking it was the woman I kicked back, but didn't get free. As soon as I saw what was waiting for me, I almost wished it was the girl. I saw a decaying corpse, alternating between patches of skin, to muscles, and the occasional flash of bone. He had one pure white eyeball that was hanging out of his skull, and an empty eye socket. I rolled out from it and threw up.

Then I saw a maggot crawl out of the empty socket, and threw up again, his hand was sticking out, and on it... My watch... I wondered whether to take it, something familiar to take with me, but If I wanted I would have to touch that... Corpse. After a moment of indecision I tried to pry it off him, but no luck. I gingerly placed my foot on the corpse's head and pulled again. This time my watch came free, along with a smattering of decaying flesh and muscle. I hurriedly wiped myself down, and pulled the watch off my watch. I put it on, but not before wiping it down with my sweater. It gave me small comfort.

I laughed as the blood, muscle and flesh splattered onto Alex before deciding it was time to lead my dirty blonde victim to his next little gift, his wallet. I whipped a piece of broken wood that had fallen off of the broken window pane just past his head while remaining hidden from his sight, trying to make him realize it was time for him to leave this room. I made sure the moment the piece of wood hit the wall behind him that the basement door slammed open, following it was a cry for help for a bit of encouragement.

I looked at my watch, expecting to see the time and date, but it was completely blank. This was no time to mourn over the little victory I was hoping to get, as I heard the sound of something in the corpses' room. I ran away and got lead downstairs until I was sure we were underground, I could smell the earth from between the flimsy wooden boards.

I smiled as I watched him enter the basement, I slammed the door behind him and locked it from the outside so he couldn't leave until I opened it. In every corner of the basement was the decaying corpse of an animal, with lines of blood connecting each of them, making an "X" on the floor. In the center of the "X" laid the body of a girl who was reported kidnapped a couple of days ago. I had left her there like this just for this occasion. Sticking out of the little girls stomach was Alex's wallet, which I turned just enough so he could see his license. I had made sure that he couldn't get it out of her stomach unless he tore it out, which would kill the girl in the process. "Have fun" I said just quiet enough not to wake the girl but loud enough for him to hear, chuckling as I did so.

I walked into the basement with my eyes closed tightly shut, not wanting to see any more corpses, I walked about 20 feet before bumping into something smelly and wet and furry. I opened my eyes instinctively, and what I saw there almost made me faint on the spot. Hanging from a noose was a Golden Retriever puppy with its fur all matted and red with blood, its entrails spilling out of a gash vertically overseeing its whole underbelly, I looked to the left, as to not see that, and saw three more puppies hung.

I fell to my knees and broke out in tears. I noticed that blood on the floor seemed to be all running toward one point, and there, besides me, was a little girl reported missing a few weeks ago. She was breathing faintly, and it looked like every inhale took all she got. Sticking out of her stomach was my wallet, I could see my driver's license. I had to make a choice, recover a piece of myself, and sanity, or keep a little girl alive. She turned her head to face me...She gargled something out, probably a cry for help, but her throat was to badly damaged to make any coherent words.

I brushed her cheek softly with my hand. I tried to hold back the tears, but they just came rushing out. The look in her eyes said she would beg for help if she could, but can't. And I couldn't take her with me, she was bound with thick rope. Even if I did manage to free her, she would slow up both up, and neither of us would be sure to get out alive. I tried to convince myself this was better for her, she was obviously suffering, I reached for the wallet, but the look in her eyes stopped me, she gurgled out something, and another stream of blood ran down her face. I closed my eyes and reached for it again, but couldn't do it.

Finally I steeled myself, grabbed it, and tore it out. The dying noises of that innocent girl would haunt my nightmares for the rest of my life. I immediately regretted it, had I just killed a girl over a wallet? She would have died anyways...I thought to myself, as I slipped that bloodstained wallet into my pocket, not sure If I would make it out sane, or alive.

I unlocked the door to the basement before dragging one of the hanging puppies up the stairs, and into the kitchen. Alex's keys on the puppies collar, making them jingle with each step the puppy is dragged up. I let him see me this time, let him watch my black hair flow behind me as I dragged the mutt around. I knew he would want his keys and I assumed he would want revenge for what he was just forced to do. All I needed was the right trap. The moment I reached the kitchen, I hung the puppy by the noose from one of the ceiling pictures before using the dogs blood to scrawl a quick little message on the wall. "I have one more thing of your upstairs, use the black key to open the door to get it back. The room with the lights on is the one you are looking for." With that, I ran upstairs and waited for him, unable to control my laughter.

As I left the basement I wondered who could be cruel enough to do something like this. The last moments of that little girl's life, the life I ended, kept playing in my mind. I wanted out! I looked up and saw the girl dragging one of the puppies across the floor at the end of the hallway. I hurried after her as quickly as I could anymore, I didn't care If I died, I just wanted revenge! When I turned around the corner she disappeared into, she wasn't there, but instead, a message written in blood. I could barely read it due to the tears and the rage, and I spotted my keys on the collar of the puppy.

I almost snatched them off, but then withdrew my hand. I softly closed the eyes of the puppy, and undid the collar it was hung by. I undid my keys from the collar, and feeling empty, turned and walked upstairs. I walked up the stairs feeling detached from life, as if the smallest wind could knock me down. I numbly opened the lock with a black key that was on my key chain, walked in, and looked around. It was a big stone room, with a single light bulb in the dead center, and a mirror on the wall I was facing. I looked in the mirror and saw the girl, looking just as tired as I was.

I locked the door behind him and smiled at him "Hello, Alex. How are you tonight?" I uttered, trying to sound cheery.

"What do you want? Haven't you tortured me enough already?"

"I simply want to talk, and I don't know, have you tortured yourself enough tonight, murderer?"

She had hit me right where it hurt. "At least I haven't descended to your level," I spat.

"Oh, you haven't? Shall we review what you have done tonight then? You woke up in a forest, you came into this house. You tore off a corpse's hand to get your watch back, you ended a young girl's life to get back your wallet, and now you are in here. That does not sound like you are a saint, now does it?" I taunted him.

"She would have died anyways, I put her out of her misery" I spoke without conviction.

"Oh, do you have a doctorate in medicine? No? Then how can you be sure?" I spat in return.

I shuffled uncomfortably "she wouldn't be... Never mind that! You're the real scum here, you put all these people and animals in this position!"

"Oh, did I? Alex, look at what you are speaking to. Say what you are speaking to out loud. I dare you." I said with a giggle.

I paused. "You're just a psycho!"

"That may be, but you still haven't said it. Alex, what are you speaking to? You are in a locked room with only one light bulb and you are speaking to a what?" I said relentlessly, trying to get a point into his head.

I moved my hand, the girl mirrored my actions instantly. "This is some sort of trick! You're some sort of demon!"

"Say it, Alex. What are you talking to? That is all you need to do and I will explain myself." I said, copying every action he did, speaking in his voice now.

I grasped my head with both hands "Get out of my head!"

I copied his actions "You are talking to a mirror, Alex. You know what a mirror reflects? What it is in front of it." My appearance slowly began to fade his. Same eyes, same hair, same everything.

"No" I sobbed "No, you can't be me, I would never..."

"I am you, Alex. Everything that happened tonight was done by you and for you. You did everything here, you kidnapped the girl, you murder the now mutilated man, you hung the puppies, you scrawled the message in blood, you killed the girl, you hid all your belongings. The only thing you didn't do were the footsteps, those were just hallucinations." I laughed.

I fell to the ground, screaming and crying, this couldn't be true!

"It is true, Alex. I have no reason to lie to myself. We are a psychopath and we are a murderer. You will never forget what happened here today. After this, you will always be haunted by the shadow inside yourself" I said before unlocking the door for him, letting the wind from the missing front door swing it open.

There was nothing else to do, I had to get rid of this beast inside of me before it kills again. I smashed the mirror and saw a way out. This is my salvation, this is my solution. Because of this decision I will never make nobody hurt again. This is my last thought as I plummeted toward the ground. I was finally free.

CheeseLord

Greetings. My name is Joseph, and I have been writing horror stories since September 2011. I take much of my inspiration from classic horror authors such as H.P. Lovecraft and Edgar Allan Poe. I've gone through a succession of usernames on this wiki, Weirdowithcoffee, Cheese Lord, and now Coffee Shop Corporate Raider. I have wrote over nine tales, and I am currently in the process of writing a lengthy one. I've been commonly described as an easygoing, humorous guy in real life.

My Daughter

By: Cheese Lord

I love my daughter.

She is just the right person who can help me live. Everything about her is perfect. Her silky, long, flowing blond hair, her beautiful blue eyes, her light skin. She is the greatest child I have ever had, and will have. She has the personality of an angel. I hope that she never grows up. Out of all her countless siblings, she is my favorite.

We live in a house in Reed's End Road, New Jersey. It is such a pretty house. It lights up red every night with the decorations I put outside of it. My daughter loves it. She usually ignores it, dismissing it as trash, but that's just kids for you, aren't they?

I should perhaps give some background on my daughter. Her name is Cherry. Our favorite season when we are together is autumn. When I'm with her, talking about how all the seasons seem to change so fast, everything feels better for me. I feel alive around Cherry, as well as all of my sons and daughters.

This particular night was a cold, bitter, breezy and quiet October night - just the way we like it. We were both lying on my bed, staring at the ceiling aimlessly. We were discussing nature and how the leaves on the trees seemed to die so fast around this time of year. I looked to her and smiled. She turned her head away from me, and my smile dissolved into a frown.

"Why are you turning away from me?" I asked her casually, tilting my head.

No answer.

My frown quickly sunk even farther, but then I smiled again. "How about of game of tag, my deary?"

Still no answer.

I looked to all of my other children, who were looking quite sleepy. Cherry herself was quite tired looking as well, her eyes half shut. The kiddies looked cold as well, their bodies shivering various times. I smiled warmly at them, closing all the windows, before holding them in my arms and rocking them back and forth, one by one. They were very pale in the faces, and were all very messy, with reddish liquid stains on their little bodies. Silly little kiddies, always forgetting to wash up.

DasFactionnaire

Guten Tag. You can call me Factionnaire...if you want to that is, ahem. I've been writing stories for a long time, and I discovered creepypasta a few years back. At first, I didn't like it, but later I started to appreciate how original and unconventional many of them are. So I joined the community, and tried my hand at writing some. My stories try to include some psychological elements and memorable, sufficiently ominous antagonists, even if they're not nearly as frightening as others. I'm an intellectual guy who's initially taciturn, but once you get to know me, you'll learn I can be quite talkative and weird by most people's standards, but nice. I like reading, writing, and drawing, even if I'm not that good at the latter.

Roark

By: DasFactionnaire

I took up work at a convenience store over the summer. It's within walking distance, my coworkers are reasonable, and the paycheck puts bread on the table. What's to complain about? Certainly not the job itself. The road I have to take to get there, on the other hand...

It wasn't so bad at first. I would walk down Hazelnut Way to work at half past eight in the morning. I had never been on the street before it became part of my daily routine, but it seemed like an OK route to work. The street was always quiet, as there were few passersby & the only structures there were a few small abandoned buildings, and the sunrise would be a good view from the street at that hour. Coming home from work, the road was still as nice to walk on, even if the sun was lower in the sky.

Then came winter, and I felt that the street's welcoming feeling had worn off, giving way to a far less pleasant feeling. Whether it was sunny or cloudy, morning or late afternoon, Hazelnut Way would give off an eerie vibe, and I started to feel like I was being watched as I walked down the road. This uneasy feeling about Hazelnut Way only kept growing, and eventually, I decided to share this with my shift mate, who proposed what the problem might be.

"It might be seasonal affective disorder. You know, where your mood is affected by the season. If you've been feeling weird since winter started, then that should explain it, right?", she suggested at the end of our shift one evening, as an aged man who frequented the store walked in.

"I don't think so, my mood hasn't changed overall, it's just a really nervous feeling that I get when I go on this one street", I replied.

We went our separate ways for the night, and once again, I found myself with an uneasy feeling in the pit of my stomach as I walked down that dreaded street to get home.

I jumped when I heard the crunching of snow behind a snow bank a few feet away, and whatever made the noise sounded rather large. Just to reassure myself that the street was safe, I cautiously walked over to where I heard the sound.

There were no people, animals, or even footprints on the ground, and I was about to turn around when I saw a pistol on the ground. It looked slightly outdated, but for all I knew, it could still be functional. I didn't want to leave a gun out on the open where a kid could find it or something, so I grabbed it by the sleeve of my sweatshirt and went to the local police station to turn it in.

After an officer asked me where I found it, he told me he'd send it to Forensics to dust for fingerprints. "When you get the results, can you tell me about it?" I asked. The officer gave me a weird look, but said he would. And with that, I headed back home at last.

The following Saturday, I returned to the police station, where the officer told me what Forensics found out about the pistol. Apparently, it had belonged to Leroy Van Tiel, a high-ranking member of a local gang in the '70s that had constantly dodged arrest. He thanked me for turning the gun in, and I asked him for more information on the gangster.

"Go to the library, look through the newspaper archive, and search for anything from, ah, September 1977 to

February 1978. I don't know what you see in this that's so interesting, though," the officer said, flipping through the police records.

Having had no work that day, I went to the library and did my research on the gangster and why his gun might have been in a snow bank forty years after his criminal days ended.

According to some newspapers I found, there was this small but significant gang that lasted for only five months in the seventies, and its whole gimmick was kidnapping random citizens and charging a ransom for their release. I kept reading the articles, and saw that in November 1977, two notable gang members, Leroy Van Tiel and "Shrapnel" Nelson, were on the road with some captives they were about to dispose of when the local police force found out what they were up to, and sent officers to drive after them.

The chase lasted almost an hour, and the police eventually lost the gangsters. One witness stood up and claimed to see a Mazda RX-5 with at least two suited men in it speed away from a large snow bank on Hazelnut Way on the night of the chase. The police went to the street, and the witness pointed out the snow bank in question, but no evidence was found, and the constant snowfall of that particular season covered any footprints that may have been left on the night of the chase.

The situation became stranger when "Shrapnel" Nelson turned himself in to the police in January 1978, claiming he left one of the captives in the snow bank on the night of the chase and "couldn't deal with the guilt anymore". The police put him behind bars, because while no one was found in the snow bank, his previous crimes cost him prison time. Nelson was very cooperative throughout the whole ordeal, but he wouldn't disclose any of his gang friends' locations. Over time, many known members of the gang went missing or were found dead, as Nelson was in his prison cell.

That was all I could find on the topic, but with the information I had just read, walking on Hazelnut Way the following Monday had me more nervous than ever. I was walking home from work when I heard crunching from behind the snow bank where I'd found the pistol.

"Who's there?" I asked politely.

There was no answer. I went over to behind the snow bank as quickly and quietly as possible, finding a tattered piece of paper. It was a list, containing written names, most of which had been crossed out, and none of which I recognized. That is, until I reached two underlined names at the very bottom of the list: Shrapnel Nelson, which was crossed out, and Leroy Van Tiel.

Then, I heard sounds from a decrepit shed about twenty feet past the snow bank. Cautiously, I advanced over to the shed, and peered inside through a crack in one of the outer walls. It was too dark to make out every detail, but I was surprised to make out the aged regular at the convenience store standing in the darkness, and he seemed to be trembling slightly.

In a falsely confident tone, he said, to no one I could see, "I know why you lured me here tonight. Same reason most of my old friends are gone. You're very persistent."

He let out a nervous chuckle. "I changed my name, disguised myself, and look, you still found me." He frowned, and continued, "OK, all those years ago, we took her. We weren't going to hurt her, we didn't have any reason to take her, and all we wanted was some ransom money. Then you came along, and, apparently being really close to her, you tried to fight us to free her. That was honorable of you, Roark, but even if you were just a kid, you couldn't have expected us not to tie you up too for pulling that on us."

The regular stopped talking, probably waiting for a reply. None came, but "Roark" emerged from a dark corner of the shed and into my line of sight. He had a rather wrinkled gray dress shirt with some rips and equally shabby trousers in a darker shade of gray. His black shoes looked extremely worn, he had a long piece of piece of rope slung across his torso like a sash, and, most strangely, his head and face were hidden under a large, thick, black cloth bag. The bizarre figure folded his arms across his chest, and, though I couldn't see his face, I'm sure he was glaring at the regular, who lost his composure.

"We were going to free you, Roark, but we were in a chase that night and couldn't risk getting caught, so we dropped you in that snow bank, and didn't have time to untie your ropes or take that bag off your head! We shouldn't have left you to die, but please, just back off!" the regular burst out, trembling more than ever. Roark stared at Van Tiel.

A moment later, he uttered, in a brisk, muffled voice, "Enter the void."

Then, he grabbed his rope-sash, slowly took it off of himself, and then lunged toward the regular, rope in hand. I looked away, and when the thrashing and gagging ceased, I looked back up. The regular was motionless on the floor, but Roark was gone. I felt a tap on my shoulder.

With a jolt, I turned around to see Roark's black bag-covered face. He held out a cracked, frostbitten hand, and I remembered the list in my hand, which I put in his. He produced a pen from his trouser pocket and crossed off Leroy Van Tiel. He then handed me a folded piece of paper and left immediately. By moonlight, I read the note.

"The gun was left behind with me on that fateful night all those years ago. I knew if you found it, you would learn how I came to be. That gangster could have been eliminated much earlier, but someone who knew my story had to witness. And now that someone has seen my quest for revenge end in success, the worms of this world can fear me at last. For while I am avenged, they are not safe, and so, I give you the option to warn them."

…Which, I suppose, is why I wrote this. Picking off members of the group that left him to die one by one wasn't the end of Roark's quest for revenge, apparently. He may attack people at random, maybe outside of this town. Hazelnut Way may be his main dwelling, but I highly doubt they're his limits. As for Leroy Van Tiel, the investigation of his death by strangling has brought the gang that Roark picked off one by one to the town's attention. I didn't let anyone know I witnessed the murder or tell them who did it, though. I know Roark gave me the option to "warn them", but I worry that he was seeing if I'd dare, and if I do, he could come after me next.

The Proprietor

By: DasFactionnaire

You are walking gingerly on the black-tinged shingles of your rooftop. You have a bird's-eye view of the neighborhood under the grey sky. The belligerent drunkard next door starts yelling about some music festival being held next month. Normally this would be irritating, but you do not quite care right now. The scene fades...

Opening your eyes slowly, you lift the thick bed sheets off of yourself. The alarm you set last night has made your radio turn on; the DJ is announcing that there will be a contest for tickets to a music festival next month. You rise from your bed. It is 5 a.m. on Thursday, another weekday you will spend at work. You go through the motions of getting ready to leave, and walk out the door to catch the city bus.

Ten hours pass. You come home, exhausted as always. You throw yourself upon the sofa, and, having the energy to do little else, you turn on the television and stare at it. You aren't paying attention to what's on though; you just stare at the screen and drift into a catatonic state of thought. After hours of this, you opt to just go to bed.

You're sitting up in bed. It's dark, but you can make everything out with ease. You turn to the door leading to the hallway. In front of the door, you see a mass of misshapen lines that look like they were sloppily drawn and shaded in with a dull pencil. The mass of lines shakes slightly as you stare at it for some time; it eventually twists into what appears to be the crude outline of a featureless man. As you look at the man, the area surrounding him shakes and twists violently.

[YOUR LIFE HAS GROWN STALE ON YOU HASN'T IT]

Before you can reply, he seems to have read your mind for the answer.

[I HAVE SEEN YOUR PREVIOUS DREAMS, AND I KNOW PEOPLE'S DREAMS BECOME MORE REALISTIC WHEN THEY BECOME TIRED OF THEIR WORLD]

[I AM THE PROPRIETOR OF MY OWN WORLD YOU KNOW]

[IT IS UNDERPOPULATED, SO I AM LONELY, AND YOU ARE BORED HERE, NO?]

[YOU WILL NEVER BE JADED AGAIN IN MY REALM]

Before you can object, the Proprietor extends his arm towards you, holding out a hand as the scene fades to sheer darkness…

You wake up and climb out of bed, disregarding the unusually eerie dream you had last night. You go through the motions of preparing for work again when you stop in your tracks.

Out of the corner of your eye, you think you saw something strange outside of your window. So, you go over to your window, and you are shocked by what you find.

The neighboring apartments, the trees outside, the sidewalks, and everything else have become abstract, and everything is in negative lights. There are no cars on the streets or pedestrians on the sidewalk… only the warped versions of the surroundings you've grown accustomed to seeing every day.

You run outside desperately, hoping to see everything revert back to normal. Still, though, the buildings are crooked, the sidewalks sloped, and the whole world is in reverse polarities, with not a single other person around to be horrified with you.

"No one else; I have to face this messed-up world alone. This isn't my home, this is Hell", you gasp, dropping to your knees in the middle of the road in front of your house.

The Proprietor materializes to your left.

[INDECISIVE HUMAN, YOU INSULT MY WORLD AND YEARN FOR THE WORLD WITH WHICH YOU CLAIM TO HAVE GROWN TIRED]

He stands there for a long time, appearing to be glaring at you, until he stretches out an arm and seems to point at you. Two beings similar to the Proprietor in their rudimentary sketch-like form appear out of nowhere, lift you up, and carry you away.

Now, you sit in a small, empty corridor, immobilized in mummy wrappings, with a hellish figure appearing before you every now and again, scratching notes as it watches you menacingly from behind a door, while you try to reason with it, plead to have your world back…

Wonder Factory

By: DasFactionnaire

It sprung up overnight, and no one is quite sure who built it. The Wonder Factory. The neon sign blazed upon the hilltop just outside of the city. There were no announcements, no advertisements, nothing. One day we went to bed with a lush and forested hilltop in our horizon, and the next day we saw the sign. "The Wonder Factory". Naturally, a small town like ours was buzzing with curiosity and soon the whole town made their way up that hill to see what new marvel sat where only trees had before.

If only I could go back.... if only I could save them all. I would give anything to have stopped the townsfolk from ascending that hill that day, to have saved them. I was the only one to make it out, just me. So now as I sit here, forty-two years after the incident and ready to die, I will share with you my story. So open both your ears and your minds and prepare for quite a journey.

It began many summers ago, I was just a young man who had just moved out of my parent's house. Having lived in a small town my whole life, one in the middle of nowhere like we were, I was a bit out of touch with the rest of the world, as were the rest of the townsfolk.

So, when we saw the sign for "The Wonder Factory" we all assumed that this was something rather common in the rest of the country. No, that's not true. There were many different theories but eventually that theory was adopted by the folks in town, all fifty-eight of us. So we found ourselves trekking up the hill to see what modern marvel awaited us.

The factory itself looked rather odd. It was surrounded by an iron fence, but the iron was painted a very bright white which made it almost look as if it were ivory. The building was painted an assortment of colors, ranging from green to blue to pink to yellow, all of them bright and cheery enough, in some areas it was so bright it hurt my eyes. It was very large, massive even, encompassing nearly the entire length of the hill. Large tubes protruded from various points which led down to the ground where they disappeared from vision, presumably entering some sort of underground area. Outside of the factory stood a man, a rather tall gentleman who donned a white cape and a white top hat, standing upon a box shouting out to all the townsfolk:

"Come one, come all! Come see what lies beyond your wildest imagination! Enter the world of magic and mystery! Let your mind's eye open for the first time! Be swept away by joy and creation! Welcome to the Wonder Factory!"

Needless to say we were intrigued. The man jumped off his box and approached the front gates, placing his hands on the bars and looking out at all of us. I finally got a good look at him. He had a wide grin and emerald green eyes which the sun seemed to catch at just the right angle, making them sparkle. He had a long nose, but not crooked in any way, shape, or form and a thin moustache sat just under it, forming perfectly across his upper lip.

"So," he said in a rather sing-song voice "Do you believe in magic? Have you ever had a dream? Then come right up and see my bright and cheery Wonder Factory" With this he pulled open the gates, and we piled in to the front door. The man nearly skipped with glee towards it, unlocking and opening it, then pausing in the doorway, beckoning us inside.

We entered and were instantly filled with disappointment. We stood not in a room of magic and wonder, but in an empty room filled with dust and dirt. Soon our little crowd began to rabble.

"What gives?" asked Mr. Barkley, the towns shop owner "I thought we were supposed to see some kind of magic. This is nothing." The crowd murmured in agreement.

"My friends! You must allow the magic in! All it takes is for each and every one of you to close your eyes! Go on now! Close your eyes!" the man shouted, dancing around the room. I could see people around me began to squeeze them shut, listening to the man as he continued urging us to do the same. "Hmm, it seems someone isn't closing their eyes! Go on now! Or it won't work!" I looked around to see I was perhaps the only one with my eyes open, so I took a deep breath and squeezed them shut. "Okay everyone! Open them!"

When I did my jaw nearly hit the floor, along with every single person's in town. We no longer stood in a musty, empty factory floor, that was long gone, instead we stood in a long hallway filled to the brim with odd gadgets and devices the likes of which we had never seen. Machines purred, gears spun, it was truly a wondrous sight and the audience, including myself, let it be known we were amazed, the room filling with various ooh's and ah's. "Welcome to the Wonder Factory everyone! Let us tour!".

We followed the man to a large room on the left side of the hallway. In front of us stood a machine we had never seen before. It had a table in the center, obviously where a man or woman was supposed to lie, and various arms protruding from either side. "This, my friends, this is the Feel Goodifying Table of Relaxation!" the man shouted with a laugh. "Lay upon this table and these hands will help relax you to lengths you have only dreamed of before! Are there any volunteers?"

Many of the townsfolk eagerly rose their hands and the man skipped up and down the row before selecting Mr. Aldeer, the towns mechanic and gas-man. "This hardworking gentleman looks like he is in need of some good old relaxation!" he said, pulling Mr. Aldeer from the crowd. The man helped Mr. Aldeer lay on the table, and began working the controls. We all watched as the table began to rise, suspending him above the base. The arms began to encircle him, landing very gently on his back and stomach. As they began to rub Mr. Aldeer he let out a pleased sigh.

"It's.... it's the most marvelous feeling of my life!" Aldeer said with the glee of a schoolchild. The audience, including myself, began to clap, cheering the Wonder Factories first invention. Suddenly, however, my head began to hurt. I jerked back and squeezed my eyes shut, to be met with screams of extreme pain and suffering. I opened them to see Mr. Aldeer suspended above the crowd that stood in a musty room, with viscious metal claws ripping the flesh from his back and stomach, the blood and entrails falling onto the cheering crowd below. But, as soon as I blinked, everything was normal. "I love this!" Mr. Aldeer shouted. I looked around to see that no one was disturbed besides me. The man skipped towards us and out of the room.

"Let's allow him to enjoy the table, and let us move on to see more magical creations!" the man said with a grin, leading us across the hall into the next room. Here sat a very long table lined with numerous chairs. In front of each chair sat a covered plate, a bib, and a set of silverware. "This is our Good Eatery Mealifier! All of you may participate in this glorious invention! I hope you're hungry however, because it packs quite a punch!

All you must do is take a seat, place your hands on the cover of your plate, and think about your favorite dish, and your favorite dish you will eat!" he yelled, hopping on the table and guiding us to our seats. I took mine next to my good friend Alex Cooper, placing my hands on the cover and wishing up a good old porterhouse steak, something that was quite a luxury considering the time and my location. "Okay everyone! Lift your covers!" the man shouted with a giggle. I pulled off the cover and my mouth began to water.

The smell was divine, and as I looked down at my plate in awe, seeing a perfectly cooked, juicy, huge porterhouse steak under me, I began to dig in. It was delicious! each savory bite left me desiring more and more, I began gulping it down, and my steak seemed to never end! Every time I took a bite I looked to see there seemed to be nothing missing!

After a little while though, something began to taste....off. My head began to swirl and hurt and I bit down into another piece, it tasted awful. I quickly spit it back onto my plate and, to my horror, I saw a slab of rotted, moldy, maggot infested meat sat in front of me. I quickly shot up from the table and jumped back. "Is something wrong?" the man asked, skipping over to me.

I was about to ring him out when I looked back at my plate, seeing nothing but a delicious looking, tender, steak. "No I.... I thought I saw a bee..." I muttered, making up any lame excuse to cover myself up. Was I going crazy?

The man frowned and then looked at his watch. "Well! Look at that! There's only time left for one more exhibit!" the man yelled. "Whoever is finished eating, follow me!" It seemed, however, many of us were not finished eating. I wanted to get the hell out of there, but only about twenty or so joined me. "Follow me! We'll go and see the last marvel of the day!" The man gleefully said, nearly galloping out of the room and down the hallway. We were nearly jogging to keep up as he headed down the hallway, passing door after door, some of which I swear I heard faint screams coming from inside. "Ah, here it is!" he sang out.

We followed him into our final room. "This, boys and girls, is your last stop." He smiled. The door shut behind us and a dim light flickered on overhead. We stood in a room that looked identical to the one we started in, before we all closed our eyes and let the "magic" flow through the factory floor. My head began to pound, nearly making me keel over and vomit all over the floor.

"What the fuck is going on here!?" I shouted out, and noticed everyone turn to me with a puzzled look on their face. I began to hear faint screams coming from all around, looking around the room and seeing horrors beyond my wildest imagination. There was no hallway, there were no rooms, it was just a blank factory floor. I could see people being torn apart by various machines, a group of people were devouring another man who lay on the floor directly to my left, people chained to walls and the ceiling in all sorts of disgusting positions with all sorts of things stabbed into them. I saw what seemed to be about a dozen people, stitched together, dancing behind me. Hundreds of people, covering the factory in every which way, but it was completely silent. "WHAT THE FUCK ARE YOU DOING TO US!?" I screamed. Everyone began to back away from me as I fell over from the wave of nausea and the pounding of my head.

"You don't see the Caring Lovatron?" the man asked with a frown. I began to cough and gag in response. "Oh dear...." he whispered. "Everyone! everyone! Please enjoy this machine! I will return shortly!" he shouted and picked me up, carrying me to the factory door. I tried to cry out, to strike him, to struggle free of his grasp, but I found myself to weak to even move. Instead, I could only watch as he opened the doors, and fainted as he led me outside. When I opened my eyes I found myself laying on a lush, heavily forested hilltop. I looked around and shot up, remembering where I just was. The man stood before me, holding a small black briefcase. "You're honestly the first to see through it all my friend." He said.

"What the fuck are you talking about!? What the hell did you do to them!?" I screamed. He simply lifted the briefcase and patted it.

"They're right here, they'll always be right here." he smiled. "They can live forever here my friend, their souls forever trapped. How else would I power the Wonder Factory?"

I staggered back, unable to comprehend what I was hearing. The man simply shrugged and tipped his hat, walking away into the forest where I would never see him again.

I never told my story to anyone, just moved on to another town and pretended it never happened. It sounds rather crazy, and I for some period of time I thought that perhaps I WAS crazy. But that can't be the case, I know what I saw. I know what awaited me. This is why I warn others, be careful what you wish for, be careful what dream you might have. You just might get it.

So that's my story, take it or leave it, enjoy it or not. Like I said, I'm not sure why I wrote it, perhaps it was a warning, perhaps it was just the ranting of an old man. Still, I occasionally think I see that big neon sign in the distance, and maybe someday I will. Maybe someday you will. I guess nothing is certain in life, not even death.

Dramaticus

Hey! My name is Zach (Or Dramaticus on The Creepypasta Wiki). I hail from a small town in Minnesota and I have always had a love for all things horror. I currently live in St. Cloud and I go to the university there and study physics and philosophy. I sing vocals and do electronics in a band called Twenty to Thirty Very Large Eagles and I love to be creative. I do a lot of work with digital art and I remix songs for fun. Writing has been a passion of mine ever since I was in grade school. I have one cat named Wobbles and he is my favorite thing ever and that cat is my only solace in this chaotic world. I am not as messed up as my stories are, a lot of people seem to get that impression sometimes, but I really am just a normal guy like you. Anyway. I hope you enjoy The Cleansing and the rest of the stories in this book.

The Cleansing

By: Dramaticus

I had never given much thought to how I would die. Maybe it was because I had spent most of my life thinking about how others would die. Especially my mother. She never understood the elaborate intricacies of my mind. And now she never will. But her voice never stopped ringing through my mind.

Constantly… Constantly… The sound of her shrill voice constantly pounds through my mind. The only way to stop the sound is to silence it with blood.

My name is Roger. Roger Gail. I am a physics teacher at the local high school. I have a deep connection with my mother. She's a bitch. A horrible woman. She "Cleansed" me every day I came home from school.

I wasn't allowed to do extracurricular activities. They were unclean. I wasn't allowed to have friends. They were unclean. Every goddamn part of my life was unclean. I was never good enough for my mother. Never. But mother protected me from the world. The world was dirty. The world is dirty… Yes… Dirty. The filthy unclean feelings I get when I lay in my bed. I don't need the touch of anyone. All I needed was Mother. Yes. Mother. When I have those feelings, special feelings, I think of mother, and I am soothed. With every drop of blood I spill, a pleasure unlike any I've ever known.

Every day I'd come home from school to, "Roger! You have been a dirty boy today. Time for your bath!" Bath. Such a horrid word. Mother would always make me sit in the bathtub and she would pour bleach onto my naked flesh… She would begin scrubbing my body with steel wool and bleach, and then I would begin scrubbing. I was filthy, and I needed to be cleansed. "Now don't worry, son. This won't hurt a bit." She would say that every time. Then she would scrub my face. The burning pain would sear my eyes. But it was okay. The pain was good. The pain was clean. The pain was always followed by the pleasure. Mother would scrub every inch of my body until she reached… My center. My center would tingle as she stroked me with her pointy, pale fingers. I never minded. This was my reward for being clean.

My life at the school was like that of any other child. Nobody ever saw what a fucked up kid I was. Mother never brought me to the school in fear of becoming filthy, so I walked to school. The path I would take was through the forest near my house. Dark, quiet, a silent tension of danger and lustful vengeance was suspended in the air of the forest. I love the tension. Gave me the biggest fucking hard-on ever. I never gave a fuck if I was late to school. No one loved me. No one gave a flying fuck if I lived or died! No… No… Mother loved me. That's why she cleansed me. Every day. The cleansing.

Every day I would await my cleansing. When I was 17, I came home one day, awaiting the pleasure and pain of being pure. "Mother, I'm home…" No answer. As I walked down the hallway to my bedroom, I began hearing a thumping. A loud, thunderous thumping. The noise was originating out of Mother's room. I had never heard such a noise.

"Mother? Are you alright?" I tentatively asked as I entered the room. Was Mother okay? Was she alright? Was she being hurt? Wh-what was going on? Why was that man ramming his body into Mother? Who was this man?! What were these sounds coming out of Mother?! Oh God the sounds. I needed them to stop. Make them stop!

I made them stop. Over above Mother's dresser was a large metal crucifix with a pointed end on it. Mother was incredibly religious. That dumb cunt would believe anything. I removed the crucifix from the wall and ran towards the man with its pointed end upward. Before the man had any time to scream, or even whimper, I beat him senseless with it. I just kept hitting him and hitting him, blood and eventually brain matter were splattering all over onto my body, the walls, and on Mother. The dumb bitch was screaming her head off in terror. I didn't mind. I finally took what was left of the crucifix, the statue of Jesus had fallen off of it, and pierced the cross into the man's eye socket.

"Roger! What the hell is the matter with you?!"

Mother… Oh Mother. She would get hers eventually. But the man was still breathing. Still a glimmer of hope that his fragile, filthy life would survive. No. I would make sure his dirty life never saw the light of day again.

I grabbed a hold of his loose limbs and dragged his mangled body down the staircase. Each thud on the wooden staircase cracked a deeper wound into the fuck's head. Blood spread like water flowing down a sewage drain down the stairs. I thrusted the body into the kitchen. A deep murmur of pain escaped from the distorted, swollen body at my feet.

"Shut up you fucking bastard! How dare you defile Mother!" I grabbed his bloody, greasy black hair and rammed his skull into the table, shoving the crucifix farther into his brain. The squish sound, the smooth entrance, it was all I could do not to scream with pleasure. I felt my center throb. I needed to finish. I couldn't stop now. I grunted as I opened the fridge door, shoved the fuck's head into the shelves of the fridge and rammed the door shut, over and over, just like he rammed Mother. He would no longer ram her. No one would. Blood spilled all over the floor and I felt the pleasure I so desired. The inescapable moment of passion was almost too much to bear.

I collapsed onto the floor. The tingling in my body finally coming to an end. But the filthy, bio hazardous mess was still left. I must clean. I took the body, and threw him down the laundry chute. Hmmmm…the body won't fit.

His large phallus got him into this mess, and it would get him out. I took my Swiss army knife and began cutting off his member. The pop sound of my knife entering and the deep, tight sliding of my knife sent chills of joy down my spine. Once I finished, the body slid down the chute. I calmly walked downstairs, hands shaking, and shoved the body into the dryer. High seemed like a good setting. Once I heard the mangled corpse rumbling around, I went up to Mother.

"Mother, it's time for my bath."

Oh, Mother. So naïve. As I undressed for my bath, I noticed Mother's hands shaking as she prepared the bath. She scrubbed my body raw, harder, and harder. I closed my eyes, dreaming of the feel of blood and metal sliding through my hands.

"Alright, Son. You're finished."

WHAT?!?!?!?!? THAT BITCH WAS NOT DONE WITH ME YET!!! NO!!! HOW DARE SHE?!?!? No! No… No… I would get my pleasure, one way or another.

I grabbed at her hair and slammed her face into the side of the tub. My arms tensed and trembling. Blood and teeth spatter around the baby blue tile floor.

"You dirty, filthy whore. You will not treat me this way. I will get what I want." I ran downstairs naked and wet. I reached into one of the kitchen drawers and grabbed the pliers. I felt light as air as I climbed the stairs slowly back up to the bathroom. Upon entering the room, I took in my surroundings of blood, teeth, and anticipation. I was ready for this. I would be in charge now.

I reached down and lifted Mother's unconscious head and pulled her into my lap. Her soft, graying hair brushing against my throbbing genitals. I needed more though. MORE! I jammed the pliers into Mother's mouth and began twisting and ripping out her teeth.

The popping sound of teeth sliding out of her old, withered, decaying gums. Blood mixed with saliva dribbled out of her mouth. Her mouth was left as an empty cavern of warmth, wetness, and wild pleasure. I held Mother's head softly and slid her mouth onto my throbbing shaft. Oh the pleasure. The warmth. The blood. Ugh, all that blood. Yes. Yes. I felt my body lose control as I started to thrust deeper and harder into her mouth.

I felt the back of her throat close around me. NO! I needed to go farther. I pulled my slimy, quivering shaft out of Mother's mouth and dug the pliers into the back of her throat. I rammed, and jammed, and thrust, and penetrate. Once I felt her spine, I opened the pliers, squeezed them onto the rough bone, and yanked with all my might. The crack of the bone, the twang of the spinal cord breaking, Mother's body jolting as her spinal cord disconnected her conscious. I threw her to the ground, got over her mouth, and thrust deep into her mouth, harder, harder, harder!!!!! Uuughhhhh! I collapsed down onto the ground, ooze dripping out of my descending member. The blood surrounding me was like a blanket of comfort. I laid my head on Mother's cold chest, and fell asleep...

Dubiousdugong

Hello. I'm Richard, though on the wiki I'm known as Dubiousdugong. I've been a member of the wiki since February 11th, 2012. I was referred to the site by a close friend and I've been in love with the site ever since. I'm a big fan of anything horror related and this site has definitely fed my hunger for the creepy and macabre. My favorite type of story to write is anything that could actually happen. Pastas of Plausibility.

As much as I'm into the dark arts, however, people tell me that I'm a nice, easy to talk to kind of guy. My only hope is that one day I'll be that person they tell me I am. I hope you all enjoy, and I hope my work is given the honor of being in such a prestigious anthology.

Gündschau Effect

By: Dubiousdugong

The Tapes

When Hitler invaded Poland in 1939, no experiments were happening. Starting with the taking of a small Polish village however, that would change. In 1940, there was an experiment lasting five days in duration known as the Gündschau effect. It tested the human drive to live if tempted with gluttony and delicacies. The scientist, respectively named, was killed by a colleague shortly following the experiment, but he audio logged each day - reasons unknown. Below are the original tapes, translated by the allies as evidence to the Nuremberg trials. Warning: the following contains graphic content.

Day 1

This is Doctor Claus Gündschau. I am accompanied by my colleagues Doctors Viktor Übelgrentz and Josef Wehrmein. Today is the start of a five day experiment to see if gluttony will preside over self-dignity. We have four subjects: 2 large Polish men, a pregnant woman who is due in three days, and a daughter of one of the men, aged four. We fed them roasted boar for dinner, and gave the men Germany's finest wine. The subjects reacted as expected; Overjoyed and surprised. Little do these humans - if that's even what they really are - know, they will be faced with nightmarish moral dilemmas.

Day 2

All four subjects were here this morning. They were served buttermilk waffles for breakfast, with orange juice and milk to accompany. Bacon, eggs and sausage were also served. It was 1:30 p.m, central German time, when both of the male subjects were given their first task. They were each given a knife. Their goal was to fight to the death. Should they have refused, they would both be shot. Should they have terminated any of the other subjects, they would be tortured then shot. As expected, they cooperated. Ironically, it occurred, the father of the girl lost. The woman and the girl were both crying during, so we had to turn the microphones off. The man's body was hauled away by the guards. The remaining three ate roast stew for dinner. Let's just say *chuckles* there was an extra ingredient.

Day 3

Subjects woke up this morning. Each were given cheese croissants with butter to dip in. Although considered, no drugs were injected in the male throughout the night, given this is a purely mental experiment; no variables allowed. The male's test was administered at 3:35 p.m, central German time. A doctor on call entered the room, and assisted the man in giving a premature C-section. The man, thinking her water broke, complied. The doctor left a bag on the table after birth. We then instructed him, in private, to extract the infant's heart and consume it. Considering the alternative, he agreed per our forceful persuasion. Entering the room, he opened the bag. Not revealing the contents to the mother, inside he found a wide variety of surgical tools. After what appeared to be a prayer, he took the child and struck it in the chest.

Accordingly, it died instantly. He then cut open its chest and pulled out its heart, still beating. He then stuffed it in his mouth whole, chewing and crying as the baby continued to sputter blood, post mortem. We had guards remove the infant's torso as the man tearfully explained to the distraught mother. From a personal standpoint, I don't see what all the ruckus was about. The little pig had it coming.

Day 4

Three subjects remained, the mother having survived thanks to an emergency operation after the man's trial. She was physically intact but mentally altered. She started mumbling to herself, and showed no emotion whatsoever. Electroshock therapy was considered, but deemed unnecessary. Subjects were served cheddarwurst. At this point, the cuisine was the only thing keeping them going. The female was given her first and final tasks. She agreed without retort, which was unusual. First, we had her incise the word "slut" on her breasts. Then, providing proper tools, we asked her to cut up her own feces and ingest it. I'll admit, we had a little fun with her during experimentation. It is noted that she did so without showing pain or disgust, most intriguing. We then had the male do a trial for the day. He was to take the frozen corpse of the infant and beat her to death with it. Ruefully agreeing, he did the job, the woman not even twitching. The little girl, as predicted, was beside herself. Something unexpected happened after the test, though. The man comforted the remaining girl, explaining as best he could the confinements of the situation. Such will be the irony of tomorrow's test. Two subjects remain. Side note: Over the course of the experiment, this male has shouldered the mental workload, yet he remains unaffected. Perhaps he emotionally detached himself from the situation entirely. Hm.

Staff note: Doctor Übelgrentz attempted to murder a guard today, so, in coordination with protocol, I shot him. Doctor Wehrmein remains firmly committed.

Day 5

Neither subject slept. Distraught by the events preceding, they held each other, hoping to live. They both were treated to France's finest crêpes for their final meal. The male was given his final task in exchange for falsely promised liberation, as this was the only way we could get him to do anything. He was to perform sexual intercourse with the girl, in all orifices. Agreeing, this time with no apparent regret, he went in and committed the act, leaving her barely alive. We then provided him with a hacksaw, then told him to saw her in half, starting with the legs. He did so, not reacting to the girl's screams, and then he finally went mad. Taking the hacksaw, he cut his head in half the entire way. This is almost medically impossible to commit, assuming his brain would give out before he could finish.

Concluding Statement

It seems that as a result of broken promises, that it only takes the followed promise of survival to drive these murderous animals to anything. This confirms both mine and The Führer's thoughts: Under controlled circumstances, man will eat his own.

The Stepmother

By: Dubiousdugong

Molly was the most charming 10-year old you'd ever meet. A pair of the bluest eyes stood out beside her locks of wavy, brown hair. On the A honor roll and an experienced violinist for her age, it may seem like she had it all. But unfortunately, such was not the case.

Her mother died at childbirth, so the only parent she ever knew was her father. This caused the two to become very close. She knew that her father would give the world for her, and she loved him very much.

One day while walking home from school, she thought she saw someone different inside her house. Her curiosity aroused, she climbed on top of some sturdy boxes to see this mysterious individual.

She was a woman, very tall. About 5'8, to be exact. She had bright, blond shoulder length hair and piercing green eyes. Molly saw this woman talking to her father, so naturally she was excited. The two of them were holding each other, laughing and sneaking a kiss every now and then. Her thirst for knowledge now quenched, the little girl went inside.

The woman greeted Molly, knowing her by name. The girl's father had to run an errand, so the girls had each other for company.

"Hello there," she said warmly. "I'm Stephanie. What's your name, darling?"

"My name is Molly. Are you one of my father's friends?"

Sensing the child's acute intelligence, she laughed a little. "Well, you see, Your father and I are getting married in two weeks. Now he had meant it to be a surprise, but it'll be our little secret. Alright?"

Molly agreed to keep quiet about it, and went on her merry way. But she sensed something wasn't quite right about this woman. She seemed nice enough, but she seemed happy - a little too happy. But, she thought, everything is not what it seems. Dismissing it as an irrational fear, Molly lived and let live, happy that her father had finally found the one.

FOUR MONTHS LATER

The brisk cool of fall was setting in. Leaves started to fall on the ground, and school was just around the corner. Molly's father and stepmother were happily married, although something strange started to happen. Ever since her stepmother started living in the house, she would have the most grotesque nightmares. Every single time it was the same. She saw a woman with gray, decaying skin standing in her closet. The woman had the sickest, most maniacal laugh the poor child had ever heard. And every time Molly screamed, holes would materialize in her chest, and she'd be dead.

The next day, Molly was in her classroom. Her face was red from crying because of what had happened that day - well every day for that matter - at recess. She would try to play with the other children, but she was met with the same result at every attempt: Ridicule. As smart and pretty as she was, none of the other children wanted to play with her. They thought she was smarter than normal, like she wasn't human. So everyday she sat alone, wallowing in her sadness with no one there.

While in class, she noticed something that caught her eye outside of the window. A necklace, as it appeared, was sitting in the middle of the green expanse of plain. As soon as the bell rang, she went outside and picked it up quickly, before anyone could take her newfound novelty.

She ran home. Looking behind her, she saw a hooded black figure shadowing her. Its pure, white eyes had a supernatural glow, and it seemed to float. She burst into the house crying, into her father's arms. When asked what's wrong, she pointed at the supernatural presence, now gliding to her room. Her father didn't see anything, and secretly worried about her.

That night she found the figure by her bedside. Before she could react, the figure placed a soft, feminine hand on the girl's lips and whispered "Shhh."

"It's ok," the soothing voice replied. "I'm not here to hurt you. I'm here to help."

"What's your name?" Molly asked, mesmerized.

"I have no name," the cloaked entity replied. "I am an angel. I lead people to the resting place. But, since you have found my necklace, I have come to your aid. Take this."

In her hand she held the same necklace Molly had found earlier that day. It was adorned with a pure white stone. Molly thanked the spirit that called itself an angel, and put it on.

* * * * *

Two weeks had passed without incident. Molly's nightmares vanished, and so had the kind spirit. She felt its protective presence so long as she was wearing the necklace. But one night, the figure appeared again, to deliver a message.

"Molly, are you glad that your nightmares are gone?"

"Yes. Thank you so much, but how come I can see you tonight?"

"I am before you to bode a warning. There were monsters that plague your dreams, but they are not what you should fear. The monsters you should fear are the ones you can't see. The ones that you notice day in and day out, but never see them for what they truly are. The monsters that plague reality. Remember, not everything is what it seems." As it said the last sentence it motioned towards the door.

Her mother stood there, both hands behind her. She smiled, but it scared Molly. She was twitching and shaking, eyes widened like a madman. Molly nervously asked what she wanted, and was granted with this monotone response:

"Molly, we haven't spent enough time together. But it's OK because now, we'll be together - forever."

Molly never heard the gunshot that killed her. When her stepmother fired the gun, she laughed.

In that same, sick, maniacal, cackle.

FantasyPhantom

"Hello there, I'm Kyle from Indiana, otherwise known as FantasyPhantom. Most of my writings are based on things that happened to more or things that I have taken inspiration from. I've always loved things horror, unorthodox, and off the beaten path of the current style of entertainment. Coming from a talented family, I take pride in my field of creativity. Everyone of my brothers and sisters grew up drawing or building things with their hands. I take pride in my writing and musical abilities, taking every opportunity to enhance my skills.

Though my appearance in real life may be off putting to most, if you ever were to sit down and chat with me, you'll find me out to be a rather fun, philosophical, and intellectual individual. A man just as you, trying to find his place in this world. I believe, however, I'm closer and closer to that discover with every word that I write and every note that I play."

A Night on the Tracks

By: FantasyPhantom

It was a chilly November evening. The wind was quiet but ever present. I was making my way home on the railroad tracks. Cursing and mentally hitting myself for not leaving sooner, I started the trek home, the sun dipping below the horizon. My dad was going to kill me when I got back.

He always wanted me home before dark. I'm not sure exactly why though. The tracks had become familiar to me over the year of walking them; it wasn't like I would get lost. Maybe he was afraid I would get attacked by something or that I might find a white van strangely alluring. Arguing with the man was out of the question, so I did my best to stay on his good side.

Only one other time had I walked the four miles home in the dark. A similar situation that I was in now, crashing at a friend's house and waking far too late. I couldn't drive at this time, I was a bit too young and my dad wouldn't pick me up (I assume to build responsibility skills or something of the like). However, I did pick up some tricks to ease my paranoia that night, music up and eyes down. I may like the thought of night, but when stuck in the middle of nowhere in the middle of the night, I become a paranoid, shaking mess. Also, having a colorful imagination is a praised gift, and a wretched curse.

If you look around you, your imagination is allowed to dance around your surroundings, making dead trees and bushes vivid hallucinations. This is why my eyes where down. If you take in the noises, the smallest crunch of leaves or a snapping branch becomes a terrible beast that wishes only your suffering. To combat this, my music blared. The only way I got home that night was watching the dim moonlight bouncing off the rails beside me and drowning out any misconceptions about my surroundings.

Not feeling like being scolded for getting home late, I tried to race the sun as I got onto the tracks. The sun was defiant though, and fell only twenty minutes later, plunging me into darkness. A gut feeling of impending doom in the form of my dad set firmly in my stomach. Realizing this, I slowed my pace and began to tread steadily home. My previous experience kicked in. Not wanting to feel the effect of the shadows around me, I put my music in and locked my eyes to the rocky path between me. It's really a strange feeling to walk at night with not a single light for hundreds of yards. Sure, the tracks were built along a road, but the road was a good couple hundred feet away. Homes dotted along the way on one side and cornfields on either side, separating me from the homes on my right. Being November, the fields have been long harvested, leaving only rugged, torn landscape. A minor tree line on either side poorly concealed the railroad completed the pathway.

Time passed and my way only grew darker. What were once dead trees, empty cornfields, and distant houses become silhouetted with blackness and the rails gave off a familiar glow from the moonlight. I could faintly see the tree line in which my home lied. I had a long way to go. Thoughts filled my head, not of terror or the fear of being jumped by someone, but of regular problems. Well, I can't say regular, as everyone has something to preoccupy them. I had an excess amount time when I walked. Doing this gave me about an hour and a half each way to my self, the dull hum of music in my ears.

The lyrics and beats didn't really stick with me, but the white noise really does aid in my self-pity. I can only think of the wrong things. I'm not sure why, but every time I do get a chance like this, I only talk down to myself, crushing my dreams and aspirations. My greatest enemy is myself. It's a mindset that I can't seem to rid myself of. Maybe this is why I lose confidence in situations like this. The darkness. These thoughts brought me back to reality, as I realized I was still in the shadows. Clouds had begun to slowly set in above me, making the path fade even further. The hue given from the rails dimming, making my path even more difficult to traverse, regardless of being a straight shot.

A feeling crept up on me. Subtly at first, but becoming ever present with each hallowed step I took. The tree line began to thicken, as I was near a mile from my home. I no longer felt as if I was safe. My strategy of avoiding my imagination waning and it began to take hold. Silhouetted tree limbs blurring with the rest of the surroundings. They looked as if fingers, waving slowly in the chilly night breeze, however they lacked any and all color. The rocks seemed more flat to me, losing the distinguished texture each had before.

Once warmly lit homes in the near distance extinguished as the trees on my right blocked them out, that long lost paranoia surfacing once more. I remembered I had I knife in my left pocket and withdrew it quickly, as if something would assault me at any given moment. Strange thing holding a weapon, whether it be a knife, a rock, or even a stick, the feeling it gives some that is. It gives one the sense of comfort, as well as the thought that one could take on anything the world slung at them. It did little for me however. I gripped it tightly in my right hand, holding it at a ready stance while continuing my trek.

I was well aware of what kind of things came out at night, having run into a few myself in the wee hours of summer evenings, and the daunting sight of seeing road, or rather rail kill. It could be as harmless as a deer or a lizard or as aggressive as a coyote or a protective skunk. Possums usually didn't care too much. They simply kept walking, or tried their best to avoid any altercations. However, being me, and as terrified as I was, I wasn't about to take any chances. One day you'll run into something that isn't afraid of the sound of your footsteps or smell, but rather defensive about it.

Almost. I was almost home. Another half mile and I was in the clear. I only had to go through an area with trees on my right, and I cornfield on my left. Easy, I thought to myself, but something didn't seem right. A feeling settling deep in my stomach that something was following me. I knew I had to keep walking. Well that was my conscience mind anyway. My subconscious mind had other plans. I slowed my pace then stopped where I was. Something felt…off. I took my headphones out and tilted my head slightly to the left. I saw nothing in the field next to me. Looking forward, I saw nothing.

Only the still faded glimmer off the two rails, stretching to the horizon. My right, same story. The short trees still looking like ominous, black fingers, brushing against the air. I turned my body, but only ever so slightly to throw a glance over my shoulder. Behind me looked just like in front of me. Dark, and empty. I began a faint stride forward, my gaze returning slowly to look straight ahead. Just my mind, I thought to myself. Just about there. Only a small walk and I'd be... A noise erupted from my right within the tree line. The sound of crumpling leaves and snapping branches pervaded the air.

I near fell flat on my face as I reacted. My knife swung blindly to towards the direction of the sound. My headphones ripped from my ear and to my side in the flurry of flailing. Regaining my composure, I scanned the trees, knife in a set position. Eyes darting around I couldn't see a thing. The pitch darkness still hindered my vision. I took out my phone with my free hand and touched the screen once. The screen lit up and I used it effectively as a flashlight. Searching the area, I couldn't find a single indication of where the sound came from. I was about to put it away when I saw a strange looking object. I crept down the side of the tracks to get a closer look. My foot freed a loose stone and it rolled towards the object.

When the stone got near, the object hopped out of the way and bounced off into the underbrush. I my heart skipped a beat when it moved however lowered itself from my throat to my stomach. Just a damn rabbit. It angered and relieved me. I stood back up and made my way back to the tracks. I stopped briefly to look at my phone. No minutes. Putting the useless flashlight away, I reached for my headphones. Groping around in the darkness I couldn't find them. I had lost them when getting down to the underbrush. Cursing myself, I started walking again. Casting a glance around me, then behind me, I found nothing. Still the foreboding shadows. I sighed as I brought my glance back in front of me. My feet locked, halting me instantly. There was something in the distance.

I felt heavy, weighted. All the breath in my lungs didn't want to leave nor could I breathe it in. Out in front of me about 100 feet was an object. More of a black form. I could see it's head and part of a torso in the horizon. With the tracks going straight, nothing was hindering my vision of what was before me. It just stood there, unmoving. I didn't know how to respond to this. I dropped my knife and stared at it. It didn't make any advances on me. The deafening silence was consuming the area. I felt the feeling of being followed again only much stronger. I turned to my left to look out across the cornfield. I could see two, maybe three black dots. Behind me I could head rocks being kicked, as if someone was walking on them. I turned and saw another figure behind me, a bit further than the first. I backed away from this one. Fear began to well up in me. These things are not normal. They only seemed to slide closer, not moving their legs. I turned back forward. The one in front of me had gone so I ran in that direction.

I didn't care what I saw was or that I had dropped some things back there, at that point I only want to get home. Running in the dark was difficult in the way that it's hard to see what's around you but surprising easy to stay balanced. Adrenaline flowing in me. A flight response took a hold of me. Only a quarter mile to my house, wind rushing in my hair, and my eyes nervously observing the blurred area around me. I looked out to the field to see black figures and blobs moving about, to my right I could hear rustling leaves and something in the form of whispers. I dared not look behind me for fear of what I might see and of losing my balance. Almost there. I could see the light of my home getting closer and brighter. My home was just off the tracks. I got to the pathway I had made in the brush and weeds to my right and jumped nearly the ten feet slope down to it. It was only at this point I fumbled and fell down. My momentum carried me out of the brush and up to the edge of the street which my home lay.

It took me a moment to gather my bearings and stand once more. Wavering slightly as I stood, I hauled myself forward, not in a run, but a hindered walk. I stopped once my foot hit the beginning of the street. I felt that feeling again, only this time, it wasn't as threatening. I turned and looked up at the railroad tracks. Standing on the rail, about where the exit is, was the short shadowy figure. Sure it unsettled me to see this strange manifestation, however somehow I knew it couldn't harm me.

The streetlight was flooding at my feet. It seemed to hold me, comforting me. Me and the figure stared at one another for a minute or two before it turned and simply went down the other side of the tracks, towards the corn field on the left side, opposite to the way I came. Returning to my home, my dad was asleep, thank god, so I made my way to my room. Shutting the door and turning off my light, I jumped in bed, not bothering to even change my dirty, sweaty clothes. All I was absorbed in was that I was home once again and I was safe. The horrible ordeal was over.

Naturally, my dad was coherent, even when sleeping, and knew that I came home late. It was about a week or so before I could leave my house again. I took the same path back to town to see my friend. Though it was a little unnerving due to recent events but one has to move on at some point. I was about a mile out from my home when I hit the tree line that opened up to the road, now on the left, and the fields on either side. The lack of music annoyed me however I take the loss of headphones over the loss of my life, I thought in my crazed head.

Instead of listening to a dull white noise and tearing myself down more, I actually took in my surroundings. For the year or so that I have been making this trek, never once did I find this path more beautiful. I could finally appreciate the effects of fall on the environment. It was awe-inspiring. With fresh air in my lungs and the astounding sights around me, I felt like I could carry myself better. It felt good after so long of a down streak.

I was just about out of the heavy tree line when something caught me eye. In the morning sun, a small glint of something was sticking out of a nearby oak tree. Curious, I went over to it to investigate. When I got closer, I could see what it was, it didn't make me feel good. Stuck in the tree was my knife, my lost headphones draped over them. When I got up to it, I found out that the headphones were utterly busted, which didn't surprise me too much. I took them and shoved them in my pocket. Grabbing a firm hold of the handle of the blade, I yanked it free of the tree. Out of reaction, I felt the blade portion of the weapon, and felt something rather odd about it. I turned the knife to the sun so I could see what was on it. It was scratched, not in a damaged way, as in something was written on it, possible by a rock. I took a deep breath as I read aloud to myself.

you're never alone

Grandpa's Back Room

By: FantasyPhantom

I've only been in this car for ten minutes and my eyes are already drooping. Mommy and Daddy were talking about boring stuff and money. It was hard for me to pay attention to much of anything. Mommy thought I would get bored so before we left she had put on the SpongeBob movie. I had already seen it a hundred times and could match up the words perfectly. I was far more interested in the fields we drove past and how they looked funny when we went fast. It looked like it was smashed together but moving.

We are on the way to drop me off at grandpa's house for the weekend. Mommy and Daddy usually dropped me off for the weekends because they were busy and always said they didn't have time to take care of me. Sometimes they said they needed to do chores and stuff, even though the house was spotless. One time I asked Daddy about this and he said that it was no fib. Though I was smarter than that. I pestered him about it and he finally told me that he wanted some time with Mommy. Mommy heard this in the next room and came in shouting at me. I didn't do anything wrong, or maybe she didn't like me asking so many questions. I still cried myself to sleep that night.

I took my ear buds out that played SpongeBob's voice and asked Mommy,

"Mommy? Are we there yet?" She quickly looked at me then back at the road and said.

"No, Will. We left not fifteen minutes ago. Be patient and watch your SpongeBob movie." She replied. She sounded kind of annoyed. I slumped down in my seat, staring at my shoes. I kicked them back and forth slowly. I wanted to ask Daddy something but it felt like he didn't wanted to be bothered either.

I laid my head on the car door and looked back to the whizzing fields. Maybe, when I can drive, I'll drive so fast that I take off and start flying. I wonder what the fields would look like then. I can feel my eyes getting heavy which means I'm tired. Maybe I'll sleep the boring car ride off. Mommy and Daddy's voices started to sound funny but I didn't really care and things got dark.

A warm feeling was on my cheeks and I could hear someone calling my name. I didn't want to wake up. It felt too good to sleep. I tried to ignore them but they shook me and called louder.

"Will. William. Wake up. We're at grandpa's." Opening my eyes, I was blinded by light. The sun was out and really bright and stuff. It kind of hurt for the first few seconds but it got better. When I could finally see, we were outside grandpa's Big Ol' Shack, as he always calls it. Grandpa himself was sitting in his rusty old porch chair that he's had since World War 2 or something. I love seeing the huge house. It had a big parking area and the house itself had like a million rooms. It looks kind of small from the outside but it funny to see how big it is inside.

I hopped out of the car and walked in the grass. The grass was really green and everything and grandpa had a huge garden by the porch. There were a few trees here and there in the front yard but in the back yard, which I really really liked, there was a beautiful tree near the back fence. Grandpa calls it an oak, which I told him that that's the same name as Professor Oak from Pokémon. Grandpa shook his head at me and said something about not being up to date on what the kids are into now. It's kind of funny how much he doesn't know. I think its cause he's so old.

Grandpa waved us over and we talked on the porch for a bit. He said we should get something to drink before Mommy and Daddy left. Daddy told him that they really had to get going and didn't have time. Grandpa just responded with.

"Alright, Robert. I…I guess I'll see you later." It was weird that he called Daddy Robert when his name was Daddy. I had once asked Daddy about this and he told me it was his real name. I told him he was lying. He just laughed and roughed up my hair. It's this strange feeling I have that Mommy and Daddy are kind of, um, not there. They seem like they don't care about much of anything. That's why I liked coming by grandpa's cause though he was old and stuff he still walked around being happy and whistling sometimes.

Mommy and Daddy got into the car and backed out of the driveway, then down the road. Grandpa and me stood there and watched them drive off down the winding path that was grandpa's driveway. When I couldn't hear the car anymore, grandpa turned to me and said,

"Ready to head in?" I nodded and we both walked through the big double doors of the white house.

During my time I spent here I had lots of fun doing different stuff. I'd get to play board games with grandpa or watch TV or run and play outside. There was a neighbor girl that I was friends with and sometimes we play around the house. Her name was Sally and she was really pretty. Some of the memories with her were the best. Playing hide and seek in the huge house was our favorite game. We never really liked going over to her house because her mom was really loud and yelled a lot. Grandpa was pretty understanding of what kind of home she came from so he let Sally stay for dinner and stuff.

I had got to grandpa's early in the morning so I hadn't had much time to do much before grandpa called from the kitchen that lunch was ready. I was up in the room I stayed on the highest floor. I really liked this room because I could look out the window and see for forever. I could see the huge yard out front, Sally's house and some other people's homes and all the trees everywhere. I could sit up here all day and stare at the world. Grandpa's house was full of surprises.

I could hear grandpa's voice calling again, this time louder which was enough for me to snap out of my daydreaming. I stood up and ran out of my room and down the stairs. Jumping some of the steps always made me feel like I was a pro runner or something. I had fallen a few times but it didn't bother me that much. I finally got down from the third floor and slid into the kitchen on my socks. "Perfect!" I thought to myself, smiling a little. I ran and sat on one of the chairs around the kitchen table and grandpa gave me a plate with a sandwich and a cup of orange juice. He always knew just what to make. As I sat there munching on my sandwich, I heard a knock on the door. Grandpa left his spot from the counter and went to go answer the door.

I didn't hear anything after grandpa left the room but I was too involved in eating to care. Soft footsteps were behind me but I thought it was just grandpa coming back into the room. Then I felt something pushing on my chest. It scared me a little and I threw my sandwich down on the plate. Trying to grab whatever was on me, I could feel it was a pair of arms. Not big arms or hairy and old like grandpa's were, they were soft and kind of small. Looking behind me, I could see a straight, yellow haired girl standing behind me, hugging the chair and me.

"Hi, William!" She hugged a little harder for a moment and then let go, backing up to give me room to turn around. She had a big smile on her face.

"Hey, Sally! What are you doing here so early?" I asked her. Grandpa was coming back from the living room, which was between the door and the kitchen and went down the hall. I heard a door open and close back there. I wonder why grandpa always goes back there when I'm doing something other than hanging out with him.

"I saw you come in with your mom and dad and thought I stop by! Don't want to waste the day! We need to keep started on fun things." She sounded like she was really excited.

"Alright! Let's go play tag outside." We both turned and ran to the sliding backdoor to get to the back yard. It's not only that I was hanging with Sally that I liked; I liked seeing the bright green grass and the huge tree in the back. It looked really neat.

So we played tag for a while, running and laughing around the yard for a good amount of the afternoon. Sometimes I could see grandpa's head looking at us through one of the windows in the house. Even though I've been here for as long as I can remember, I never could find that room that grandpa went in. I think it's the same room that he kept looking at us through. It was kind of weird but I didn't pay attention too much to that.

After hours of playing different games and running around, Sally and I were tired so we went and sat by the big tree near the back to get some shade. We sat next to each other at the base of the trunk. The trunk of the tree always looked like something was splashed on it. I imagined it was whatever made the tree so pretty so I didn't really care. I would have gone to sleep there but Sally kept talking to me about random stuff. I didn't want to be mean so I listened to her. She stopped talking after a bit and lied down, staring up at the leaves. I did the same on the other side of the tree. As I went to put my head down, I felt something on the back of my head. I wasn't very comfortable so I tried to put my head somewhere else. My head once again lied on some object.

I sat up and looked at what I was laying on. I think the second one was a rock but the first one looked strange. I picked it up and turned it in my fingers. It looked kind of like a branch or something. Maybe, but it was kind of squishy. Whatever it was was about as long as one of my fingers but a bit bigger. Part of it was hard, only on a small part of it. I almost threw it, thinking it was poo or something but remembered that grandpa didn't have any pets, at least anymore and with the huge fence that went around the yard, no animals could get in. It was covered in mud and dirt so I couldn't really see what it was. At one end, it was all rough and had something in the middle. It kind of reminded me of a fi-

"William, Sally, come on in and have some lemonade." Grandpa called from the back porch. He had a different pair of clothes on than the ones I saw him in earlier. I got up and went over to Sally to wake her up. See had been so tired that she fell asleep. When she opened her eyes, I told her to come on. She stood and walked with me to the house. I dropped the thing I found, not thinking about it again.

When I asked grandpa about his clothes, he told me he had spilled some paint on them and wanted just get a new change of clothes. I looked around and didn't see anything that had a new color to it but I didn't really care. Sally and I flopped down in front of the TV and started watching cartoons. Grandpa watched for a little bit then fell asleep in his big chair. I had seen these cartoons, like, a billion times so I got bored. I tried thinking of something else to do with Sally. A thought came to me, something I've always wanted to know. I turned to Sally and asked her,

"Hey Sally, want to go look around the house?" She looked just as bored as me but also looking like she was too sure.

"Why? We've already seen the entire house and been in every room. I don't know, just sounds kind of boring." She turned back to the TV.

"Not all the rooms." When I said that, she turned back and looked like I finally got her attention.

"What do you mean?"

"I mean, you know that room that grandpa always goes when you and me are doing something?"

"Yeah..."

"And the room that grandpa looks at us from when we're out back?"

"Your point?" She sounded like she was getting annoyed.

"Let's go find that room. I don't think we've been in there and it sounds totally awesome and mysterious! " I tried to sound excited to make her want to do it while also being quiet so I didn't wake up grandpa. She sighed and said,

"Fine. It's not like there's anything on TV anyways." She got up and I followed.

I told her we had to bring something to protect ourselves, to fight back monsters in the unknown. This got her excited and we tiptoed to the kitchen. Opening the drawer, we saw all kinds of eating things. I grabbed the big wooden spoon and she grabbed the spatula. Quietly closing the drawer, we got down on our hands and knees and started to crawl down the hallway.

Grandpa didn't have the lights on now cause it was still bright outside. We didn't turn them on cause we didn't want to wake him up. There were doors on either side of us all the way down the long hall we crawled in. I started to think it was a bad idea to crawl cause my hands and knees began to hurt but I didn't want to sound like a wuss when I told Sally I was tired so I kept quiet. We finally reached the end of the hallway, which went of in two directions. To my left was nice a guest room and the bathroom and to my right was grandpa's room straight back and a sunroom to the left. I told Sally that we were going to check out the guest room first.

We searched underneath the bed and in the closet also behind the pictures on the wall just to be sure. Nothing. It kind of made me sad not to find anything but I there was still ground to cover. I still wanted to keep looking. Sally seemed to have the same idea. Our next stop was the bathroom. Sally check under the sink I checked in the shower. Neither one of us wanted to check near the toilet so we didn't. We could have missed a secret door or something behind it but it was gross so we didn't. Also, if I were a spy or grandpa, I wouldn't want to crawl around the toilet just to get into my secret hideout. That's just dumb. We left the bathroom and went the other way, towards the sunroom and grandpa's room.

We decided to hit the sunroom first. The sunroom was pretty big and old stuff everywhere. Sally sneezed a few time to all the dust in the air. I was kind of surprised to not see the dust anywhere else in the house. We couldn't find anything that stood out as old to us. The old wheelchair that grandpa had last year when he got hurt was still there. I remember I used to ask him to race me with me on my trike. He just shook his head and laughed. I almost dropped some big paintings when I was trying to see what's behind it.

The room was empty. I don't think grandpa would hide anything in this dusty old place. We grabbed our weapons and exited the room then went to the left. Grandpa room was the last place it could be. The door was shut but luckily, couldn't be locked. It was one of those doors, like all the ones in the house, that didn't have a lock on either side. I slowly pushed the door open and crawled inside.

His huge bed was the first thing I saw, he bought just before grandma passed away. It kind of feel bad for him, having him sleep in a huge bed like that alone. I crawled around it and looked in the table next to the bed. Nothing but medicine and some shiny jewelry. I don't think he wears this but he keeps it around anyway. Sally went to go check the closet and I started looking around the study area by the window. Nothing in, on, or under the chair and the table that was near it didn't have anything but pencils and paper. Sally didn't find anything in the closet and sat on the bed. The only two things left that were in the room were a bookshelf and a big standing mirror. I started checking the bookshelf when she sighed.

"Are you sure there's a 'secret room' somewhere back here? We've checked all the rooms that it could be and nothing. Nada!" She sounded angry. I stopped searching the bookshelf and went to go sit next to her.

"Sorry, Sally. I really thought I'd find something back here." I looked down at the wooden spoon in my hand that was in my lap. The room was real quiet and I thought it would last forever. Sally got up and looked at the window.

"Let's just go do something else."

"Alright." I said. I was kind of sad that I didn't find anything.

Sally started walking out of the room. I began to follow her but I remembered the big standing mirror in the other side of the bed, opposite of the door. It would bother me if I didn't check everywhere. I went over to it and grabbed on to it. It was pretty big cause it was a standing mirror and all but this thing was ginormous. It was easily as tall as grandpa and just as wide. I was hard for me to stretch my arms to reach both sides of it to move it to the side, not considering how heavy it was. I couldn't move it so I went to the right side if it and lifted forward, off of the wall. I could see something but I didn't have a good view. I whispered for Sally, but she couldn't hear me. I whisper yelled as best I could. At first I didn't hear anything. then I heard footsteps coming back down the hall.

"What is it, Will?" She whispered back to me coming back in the room.

"Come here, I think I found something." She shook her head and walked over to me.

"This better be good." She got on the other side and we both got ready to lift it up.

"On the count of three. One. Two. Three. Lift!" On three, we both lift it up and back. It was a lot heavier than I thought it was and it started to fall forwards towards us. Sally yelped and got out of the way. I tried to get in front of it to stop it from falling but I wasn't strong enough. It came down on me forcing me to the floor. Just as I thought it would crush me, it stopped. I had closed my eyes cause I was kind of scared but when I opened them, I saw that the bed had caught it, barely though. I had to crawl out from under it to see what had happened. Sally was on the other side, stuck were she was between the mirror and the wall. I was fine, but shook up a little.

"Will, look." She got my attention as she pointed to what was behind the mirror. It was a doorway, not as big as a normal big person door. It was about my height with a another foot or so high and a little smaller wide.

"Looks like you were right will." She smiled at me and reach out to open the door.

"Wait!" I said a bit louder than I wanted to.

"Let me check it out." She nodded and held the spatula close to her chest. I took out my trusty wooden spoon from my back pocket and held it at a ready position. I slowly reached out with my left hand for the doorknob, which was kind of in the door as to hide it. I tugged at it and it popped open. The door whined as it open and all I saw inside was darkness. It smelled kind of funny but it wasn't that bad. I put my right foot into the darkness, about to go inside when Sally and me heard a noise of the next room.

It was the sound of grandpa stretching and yawning. I got really scared this time and quickly pulled my foot out. I dropped the spoon somewhere inside but I was too afraid to be caught to care. I slammed the door shut and Sally started looking around nervously. I told her to grab the other end of the mirror to lift it back into position. She did and with both of our strength put together, slowly lifted it back to its original spot. I grabbed her by the hand and pulled her from the spot she was standing in and we ran from the room. I heard footsteps coming down the hall towards us and we ducked into the sunroom.

"Hide, quick!" I told her and we both ran around trying to find a spot to hide. I found a spot behind the old wheelchair and she hid in some hanging clothes. The footsteps got louder and louder until I heard them go into the bedroom. It was hard for me to breathe part from the fact that the room was full of dust and also that I was terrified of being caught. I could hear something being moved then put back in the bedroom than the footsteps started coming back this way. Sally looked at me and I looked back. We both had the same scared face and we knew we were thinking the same thing.

The footsteps came into the sunroom and I stopped breathing. Well, more holding it but still , I didn't like it. The sound slowed down as they got closer to were I was, until the sound completely stopped. The wheelchair that I was hiding behind slid out from in front of me and I feel forwards. I yelled but stopped when I saw my grandpa's happy face.

"Gotcha!" He said. He didn't sound angry at all. It sounded like he was played a game.

"Sally I see you too over there." Sally slowly moved the clothes out of the way.

"I see what you kids are doing…" This made us both freeze again.

"You're playing a game of hide and seek! Well, I found you." He started laughing and left he room.

"Alright, come on you two. Time for dinner." We both got up and looked at each other for a minute or so. We both knew what the other was thinking. That was way to close. We slowly made our way to the kitchen. Before turning the corner, I looked back at grandpa's room. I couldn't see anything moved so I guess he didn't notice. I turned the corner and side. I'm glad that didn't backfire on me.

Sally stayed for dinner cause of the usual reasons, she didn't want to go back, her mom is crazy, and she was too tired to walk anywhere. Grandpa had called her mom and asked if she could stay the night. I could hear her mom yelling over the phone but she still said yeah. We had chicken nuggets and macaroni and it was really good and stuff and I was full afterwards. After dinner, grandpa went to wash up and go to bed. Sally and me went up to my room so that I could get her out a sleeping bag. We watched TV up in the room for a while till it was about elevenish. I kept thinking about that back room in grandpa's room and what was in it.

"Hey, Sally." I asked her. She was sitting in a beanbag chair in the corner.

"Yeah?"

"What do you think is in that room?" She flipped on your tummy and put her feet up in the air.

"I don't know, what do you think is in there?" Truth was, I didn't even know what was in there. I was really curious about what was in there though. Maybe grandpa was a spy or something and his secret lair was in there or maybe he was a mad scientist with a laboratory. I really didn't have a clue.

"Not sure. I am glad that he didn't catch us snooping around in there."

"Yeah, no joke." She turned back to the TV. Sometimes I thought she was more interested in the TV than what I had to say. Doesn't matter. Now I'm trying to think if we could get caught. I knew we wouldn't but did we leave any clues? I couldn't think of any. We put the mirror back were it was and the rest of the room looked the same as when we came in. I hadn't lost anything, I don't think. Wait, what about…

"Hey, Sally. Do you still have the spatula?" She turned over and pulled it from her pocket.

"Yeah, why?" I checked my pockets and couldn't find anything but lint. She suddenly knew what I meant by that.

"You lost the spoon!?" She sat up quickly.

"I think I dropped it in the back room!" We both stood up real fast.

"We have to go back and get it! He'd be sure to find it in there!" She said and was already running out the room.

"Wait!" I ran after her. She stopped right before the stairs.

"What? We have to go get it."

"I know, but it's not like we can just run in there, through the mirror down on grandpa and grab it and we can't just go ask him if we can get it. We have to be sneaky. This has become a covert mission!" She heard this and nodded.

"Sneaky. Got it." She slowly made her way down the stairs and I followed.

We made it down all three sets of stairs and came out into the living room. Everything was really dark and quiet and I was scared but I knew I couldn't show it. We got back down on our hands and knees and started down the hall again. After we took the right turn at the end, I moved past Sally to take the lead. I told her I had this and she nodded. I made my way up to the bedroom door and slowly grabbed the doorknob and turned it.

Grandpa was snoring in bed and everything was dark. There was a light coming through the window in lines on the wall from the light of the garage outside. Sally was right behind me, trying to be as quiet as possible. We crept around the base of the bed really slow like and after a time, made it to the other side. Now, all that is left, is to move the mirror. I looked back at Sally, then at grandpa, both were equally as silent.

Sally got on the left side of the mirror and I got on the right. We couldn't lift it back or let it fall again so I told her to pull it at the bottom. I heard the sound if it dragging on the wall above and the carpet below. I pulled it enough for the door to open told Sally to stop. It was only about two feet of space between the mirror and the wall but that was enough. I reached in with my left hand and opened the door. It was just as dark as before and seemed to go on forever. I backed out of the way so Sally could go first. She looked at me like I was stupid or something but shrugged and went in. It was, again, partly for me being scared but also to so she didn't screw up shutting the door.

"There's stairs." She whispered to me from somewhere below. I nodded but realized she couldn't see and just went on to shut the door. I heard loud thuds and Sally screaming behind me. I looked back really quick but couldn't see anything. I peaked around the mirror to see if that woke grandpa up. When I could finally see him I quickly went back inside the door and slammed it shut. His eyes were wide open looking right at me.

Sally had finally stopped screaming but now was crying at the bottom of the stairs. I stood up at the top of the stairs trying to find a light switch. When I found a cord I pulled it hard. Nothing happened. I pull it again and again but it wouldn't turn on. I felt on the walls and found a light switch. With one flick, it turned on and everything got real bright. I ran down the stairs to find Sally curled up crying around the corner.

"Sally, are you alright?" I asked, looking over her to see if she was hurt.

"No…" She replied, tears in her eyes and her arms wrapped around herself. Nothing ever happened to me like this. Sure I had fallen a couple of times but Mommy or Daddy would be there to make me feel better. They weren't here but grandpa was. He had to help if he knew she was hurt. At the top of the stairs, I heard something being moved and a creaky door opening.

"Grandpa, you have to help! Sally fell and I think she's hurt! Please grandpa, hurry!" I turned the corner and say grandpa at the top of the stairs. He wasn't frowning or smiling.

His face was kind of neutral. He slowly made his way down the stairs. I look back from Sally back to grandpa. She was at the very start of the hall that made a left a bit at the end. This place did lead somewhere but I'm sure grandpa didn't want us down here.

When grandpa reached the bottom I ran up to him asking him to help. All he did was shove me a side and walk up to Sally. When he got over to her, he got down on one knee and turned her face to the light with his hand.

"I..I think s-she hurt her arm…"

He let go of her face and looked at her arm that she was holding. She held it up to him. Nothing happened for a second or so and Sally began to bring her arm back down. Grandpa grabbed on to her arm real hard from what I could see and Sally screamed. I gasped and held my hands up to my mouth. Grandpa twisted her arm in his hand and threw it to the side. He then grabbed her face once more and lifted her from the ground. I looked like it hurt a lot cause her face got all red and she was making pain noises.

He looked at her a little bit, turning her in the light before turning and throwing her the nearby wall. The sound when she hit made me sick to my stomach. She landed on the floor and stopped moving. I couldn't hear her making anymore sounds either. Grandpa then turned and made his way past me to the base of the stairs. I couldn't move from that spot. I felt real sick at what I had just seen. I look at grandpa and he looked back at me, turning and blocking the path back up the stairs.

"Think you're so tough now? Go on. You were so curious to see what's down here, go take a look. You have five minutes." He folded his arms in front of him and gave me an angry look.

A few tears made their way down my cheek as I walked past Sally. I turned back to her and grandpa shook his head and pointed down the hall. I was really scared and stuff, both for Sally and me but I made my way down the hall real slow. When I got the end of the hall it turned left around a corner and then a right into an open room. I looked back one more time to see grandpa getting closer so I quickly made my way inside the big room.

The room was kind of dark and smelled funny. I could see plants in flowerpots around the walls and some kind of weird table in the middle of the room. It looked like it was metal and something smudged on it. There was a sink in the corner along with a locked cabinet and a bin next to it. I went closer to the center of the room to get a better look at the table. It was just a plain flat metal table. On the ground I saw a ring or something. Picking it up I saw something was written on the inside.

"Love never dies." Grandpa said from the doorway behind me. That's what the ring said too. I got scared and dropped the ring.

"It belonged to your grandmother. She was always the sweetest desert flower there ever was. I remember when I first proposed to her. Had that ring specially made for her. It is true, you know, love never does die." He looked down at his feet and sighed then made his way over to me.

"She never did really die then, you know. She's still here, with us. As it is said, love never does die, only bodies do." I was getting more and more scared of the man in front of me by each footstep. He came right over to me.

"She loved you." He put a hand on my shoulder.

"And you always said you loved our garden outside, especially that oak tree by the back fence." I was getting more uneasy by the second. I had no idea what he meant.

"And did you know that I discovered something while studying down here? It's what I've been working on for the better part of ten years now. I discovered something that could put all the dead bodies in the world to use." I wanted to make a break for the door but I knew he would catch me. He walked over to a spiky plant in flowerpot on one of the tables. I think it's called a cactus.

"Humans make get fertilizer. Blood and tissue work better than any name brand product out there. Works for any type of plant too. From trees, to flowers, to even cactus'. I could make millions on this research and finally retire having accomplished something." He turned to me.

"And you could be a part of it if you wanted to, but you have to promise not to tell anyone about this yet. If you keep quiet, I could buy you all the things your mom and dad won't buy you. You and me kid." He kept playing with the needles on the spiky plant.

"What….What h-happened to g-grandma?" I slowly started walking towards the doorway.

"She was the first I wanted to try my research on. She would have wanted it. And knowing that true love never dies, I killed her. I scattered parts of her around the oak tree and water the tree every month or so with small amounts of her blood. You've noticed the trees beauty, haven't you? That tree is a wonderful and beautiful as your grandma was."

"No grandpa, this is bad! You can't do this to people, it's mean and wrong!" I yelled at him, tears forming in my eyes. He turned, looked at me for a quick moment, shrugged, and turn back to his plant.

"Be a part of my riches or my research. I don't really care, William."

I ran up to him and shoved him, all the anger coming up from deep in me. I felt so angry that he'd do something so horrible to grandma and other people. He fell forward on the cactus and let out a really loud scream. I didn't get to look at him though as I ran out the doorway and down the hall. I saw Sally and went up to her. She still wasn't moving even as I shoved her and called her name.

"You and that little bitch will be put underneath the garden by the front porch! You'll make this house beautiful!" Grandpa yelled from the other room. I got scared and ran up the stairs. When I got to the top I turned the light off and slammed the door shut. I thought of putting the mirror in front of it to slow him down but I thought of that after I was already running down the main hall.

I went out the back door to try and get out of the house to the back yard. It was really dark and the lights from the other houses weren't bright enough for me to see. I tripped while trying to get away from the house, some dirt getting in my mouth we almost made me sick. I ran to the back fence and tried to climb it but couldn't cause it was too high. I had nowhere to go and I could see grandpa looking for me in the house. Then he turned and went for the back porch door

I hid behind the big oak tree and waited quietly for him. I couldn't hear anything except a few crickets and bug and stuff.

"Let's play hide and seek William." He called from the back porch. I pushed myself up against the tree real tight so he couldn't see me or find me. His footsteps in the grass were moving all around the yard, moving from the sides of the yard back and forth. He even checked the shed but found I wasn't there. I could hear him coming close on my right so I slowly slid around the left side of the tree to be as opposite of him as possible.

I started to lose control of my breathing and started to feel real sick. Tears started up again and I could feel them on my cheeks. All was quiet for the longest time and I thought he was going to give and go inside. I slowly slide more around the left side of the tree until my back was facing the house. I breathed in deep one more time before turning around. Before I could turn though, I felt a hand on my shoulder.

"Gotcha."

The Maggot Sisters Want to Play

By: FantasyPhantom

As the night does crash,

and the moon does fall;

the clouds do clash,

and the clouds to ball.

Shelter is needed,

feet do move.

Foot after foot, impeded,

by the oppressing grooves.

Hills are high

and mud does flow.

Fluttering eyes do pass by

a home with glow.

Weary and tired,

My feet do tumble

on the rotten porch;

I do feel a rumble.

"Nothing more than a wild animal."

I think to myself,

"Simply trying to escape the rain,

attempting to save himself."

The dusty door is met

with a shaking fist.

Whoever resides here, I bet,

can't be worse than an ankle cist.

A worried and hurried voice does echo

from inside the shack.

Entering, I see a woman like a gecko

with a hunch for a back.

"You come in here

as if you weren't avoiding a fire.

Simply you can help me.

Your situation can't be as dire."

Her voice is gravely

and rittled with age.

I respond rather casually

to this woman, skin as beige.

"What has you troubled?

What has you worried?

You look positively stressed,

with eyes so pearly."

"My dear sister is gone!

Such a sweet little fella.

You must find her before dawn.

Her name is Bella."

"Where do I look?"

I say then pan around.

She points to a basement hatch.

This must lead far underground.

I cautiously open the door.

A blast of stale air hits me.

As I walk inside, she shuts the hatch.

A glimpse of her face I caught,

Nothing but shear glee.

A torch far below lights my way.

The stillness is petrifying and choking.

It's light keeps shadows at bay,

A kind of darkness, simply cloaking.

I enter the enormous room.

More a cavern than anything.

A black form darts into the gloom.

In a deep tunnel goes this...thing.

I chase after it.

I've come this far.

I dart in its direction.

Passing by walls ajar.

I come to an intersection.

No way looks good;

for all three appear menace.

I can't just sit here and brood.

My feet run, I pray for penance.

I follow the middle path.

Light does fade.

My mind is knocked for a loop.

Let me do the math.

My mind is made.

Dead end. Fuck this.

I'm done with these caves.

To escape would be a welcome bliss.

Down the corridor is a blaze.

When I arrive, all is dark.

The way I took is now blocked.

What blocks it, a wall of firm bark.

Leaving me a little more than shocked.

The original right path

now bears a light.

Rain runs down it,

like a leaky bath.

I need to be somewhere bright.

The trail leads up.

Splitting and shattering wood sounded.

I remerge at the top.

For hell I am bounded.

I am under the porch from before.

At that moment, something came clear.

Something was under here that could bore.

Something; not a possum nor deer.

Having the porch being destroyed.

I made my way back inside.

My fear filled face turned pale white;

My mind was of itself, beside.

Gruesome teeth and mangled fur.

Morphing smaller and humanistic, I concur.

The old hag came back in the room,

smiled, ran towards the creature, dropping her broom.

The beasts bloodied claws turned pudgy

Fingers became clear, clothes fitted.

The face turn smooth, make up smudgy.

Of clairvoyance she was not committed.

"Bella, my sister! You return!

How was the trick? Tricked him you did?"

The first old hag had asked with concern.

The second, matching her sister,

replied as would any kid.

"Look over there Rella,

He stands at the door!"

"Perfect! Well done Bella!"

My feet frozen to the floor.

"W-who are you two?"

I manage to squeak.

They cast a glance towards me.

Their wrinkled faces looking rather bleak.

"We are Rella and Bella,

the sisters of the wood.

Needing help from the poor few

with the courage that could."

"Tricked you we did;

your fate now sealed.

You shouldn't have answered our bid.

Mind illusions we have dealed."

"Leave you cannot.

Wander the caves you will.

Survive long you will not.

You, by your own thoughts, will kill."

"Drive you mad. Yes, yes very well.

Hear the final tolling of the bell."

"Gave us time with a rouse.

Chasing monsters in the dark.

Skin will crust, blood will bruise.

Try to live, follow the bark."

I can't take the verbal onslaught.

I exit the front; eyes closed, hands on ears.

Quiet is present, I am caught.

Within the darkness of the cave, shadows to near.

Turning, I find nothing but bark.

A shape carved into it.

An old door to a shack is there.

This is the wall of bark from before! Once bear.

For years you will wander,

the cave of the sisters.

Till madness will ponder;

your thoughts go twisters.

Eat your arms for food is scarce.

Maybe ears too, they only listen to screams.

When your weary, lay down to sleep.

Haunted thoughts and twisted dreams.

Don't wander the woods at night,

for they always are looking for fun.

The sisters both agree, never fight.

Agree to help your life is done.

As the night does crash,

and the moon does fall;

the clouds do clash,

and the clouds to ball.

Shelter is needed,

feet do move.

Foot after foot, impeded,

by the oppressing grooves.

Hills are high

and mud does flow.

Fluttering eyes do pass by

a home with glow.

The maggot sisters want to play,

their favorite game,

not in the time of day.

Death befalls those who help the dame.

You won't find them during sun

So travel at dawn, and hide at dusk.

Eventually they'll get bored, waiting done.

Witches awake and hunt.

Awake, you shall, impaled by elephant tusk.

The Seven Deadly Songs

By: FantasyPhantom

Author's Notes

This is "The Seven Deadly Songs". What is posted here is the first part of three to tell the whole tale of a misfortunate family burdened with a partners divorce, the confusion and bewilderment of an innocent young girl, and a mysterious statue along with certain tunes that revolve around it. Enjoy.

Prologue/Welcome Home

Wow. That was ridiculous...Who needs zoning for a fucking bathtub? Really? Oh well. I'm just glad to finally

get in my comfy Toyota seat and settle in for the usual mundane ride home. Pulling into my reserved spot in the Crystal Heights apartments, I turn the key to off. Slowly the car rumbles to a silent rest. I can't do anything but just sit there. I'm so done with it all. I rest my head on the steering wheel and think through my situation. I find it helps me plan things out if I just sit there and think of who I am and what is wrong with me. From there I can move in the direction I so choose. Ugh. Fine... Here I go.

Hey, yeah. What's up? My name is Andrew. Andrew Brookstone. I'm 32. Male. Duh. I live in this shit hole of an apartment with one bedroom and little luxuries. I have a dead end job with a zoning company for the Crested Butte Montana, Zoning Inc. That company has been falling through the cracks of the United States payroll for years now. Barely finding money to stay running itself, let alone its employees. Me? My job is to go to the various businesses and residential of the local area and clear or decline people to different add-ons or renovations for their home or business. You wouldn't believe the crap I put up with. I think there are only two things in the world that get me through the day. One is music. I've loved music ever since my mom hummed my first lullaby to get me to fall into sleeps cool embrace. Now I collect all different types of music; classical, rock, metal, pop, disco, rap. Anything. It all feels so good to walk through the homes of customers and take my necessary measurements and listen to the various types of artists and groves that the different tunes offer. I've got a huge TV stand (that I got for a steal at the local flee market) filled to the brim, not with a fancy TV, no, with all my CD's and records I've collected over the years. Only one thing surpasses my love for music. My love for my beautiful daughter Lilly.

Lilly is 14. She's around four foot seven, maybe. Not skinny, not fat. Average. Thank the god and his little tike that my kid isn't as big as the car I drive or so light that, with proper duck taping, could be used as an Olympic javelin. She's average in about every way you'd expect a 14 year old girl to be. Average social life, healthy mental state. However, I believe that she is the most beautiful girl out of any I've seen of others her age. All in all pretty acceptable. She's just freaking' stubborn. What more could I ask for though? In school, she has good grades. Favored by her friends. Wanted by the guys. There's only two down sides however. She dresses like shit. No joke. I go into her closet and all I see is black, red, pink, and purple. In her laundry, I spot dark colored shirts, pants and under things. Believe me I didn't pick out her wardrobe. All the clothes I bought her from places like Aeropostale and other name brand clothes of brighter colors, she simply tosses aside. Still, not a bad tradeoff. A stunning, young, polite girl that hides her beauty with a dark silhouette. The other down side is the other side of the gene pool. Janice her mother.

She was once pretty, smart, outspoken, and funny but since has turned sour and bitter. Every phone call is filled with hateful words and venom impregnated sentences. Clearly we are not together. It went down like this, in her eyes. She felt like my love for music was dumb, I was a jobless clown, hardly gets out, physically unappealing, and just overall a sloppy mess. She is, as of now, living upstate with her lonesome self in a big fancy house with those little porcelain figurines that cost about forty bucks a piece. Her damn mom and dad moved away and left her with a small bank account filled with a quarter of their savings. Ever since she's had it made. We currently are dealing with a custody battle between me and her with Lilly caught in the middle. Right now she has primary custody of Lilly and with the way things are going on this end...I...don't even want to think what will happen with her. Wouldn't you find it little unfair if you can hardly afford a lawyer to help you while she's got a high class guy whose been doing this for years and is a professional at custody battles such as this. As for anything else I might know about her? Fuck if I care... I got it hard as it is, I don't need to get deathly envious of someone who has it better than me.

Ow. My head is staring to hurt. Maybe I should get a steering wheel cover to put on this thing to make it comfier. Leopard print sounds nice, or better yet that furry pink crap you see in teenage girl's cars. Ah. That's something to lie on and relax on...Whoa. I've been sitting out here for over a half-hour. Realizing that I should probably get inside, I tighten my grip on the key with my right hand that's been resting on it for a while on and shove the keys deep into my pocket. I lazily grab my jacket and step out in to the brisk September air. I'm so out of it I barely feel me slamming my car door shut. I start walking towards my door but get snagged and stubble backwards. Are you kidding me? I look at the car door to see my jacket got caught in it. Next time...I will wear the stupid thing before I leave the car. I unlock the door and free my jacket from the merciless mouth of my car door. Now I put that thing on and start walking to the mailbox. I should really check if it came in today. I dig my keys out of my pocket and unlock the metal mailbox. Instantly I feel relieved to see the brown wrapped box sitting cozily in its room. My hands reach out and pull it out. Shutting the door and locking it and walking to my apartment all I can think of is how long I've been waiting for this to come in. I'm practically floating up to my door and breezing my way into the room. Everything I'm carrying falls onto the bed and I take the things out from my pockets as I get comfy, I'm practically made of Zen.

"Mr. Burglar? You inside already? Only a key can unlock doors that fast." A voice comes drifting down the hall into my room.

I turn around to only be more relieved and relaxed to see my wonderful daughter Lilly leaning on the door jam. Those sparkling sky blue eyes with raven black hair practically drifting around and on her shoulders. She's dressed in that damn black and dark purple again which is tensing but I'll let it slide. I mean. It's her. You couldn't turn Lilly down. She was just too cute and perfect to get angry at.

"Yes well... Um... I might have run into your dad and happened to drop all of his keys without even noticing" I reply, trying to play along.

"Well, before you make off with the only TV in the house, why don't you make me a peanut butter nd' jelly sandwich with a crystal light. Mk?" She gave a fake excited face with her mouth open, exposing her perfect teeth, and had the biggest smile you could see. I paused, looked away at my things all piled up on the bed and turned back with a smile almost uncanny to hers and said with much enthusiasm.

"*gasp* No!" Then cocked my head to the side like a cocky teenager. She scrunched up her nose and said.

"You're no fun." she ambled into the room and gave me a hug. I sighed.

"How was your day? Tell that chick to back off?" I say trying to be supportive while I put my various things away in their pre-determined spots.

"Yea, then she told me she'd 'Back off if I backed off the eyeliner' then proceeeeded to call me a gothic skank." She said without hardly any hesitation.

I fumbled and dropped my wallet on the floor during the transfer from the bed to the dresser when she said this and I looked at her with much concern for the end of this tale. "...And?" I denounce.

She shifted from one foot to the other and brushed the hair from her face. "Theeeeen I told her fine then, go back to trailer park home and do something useful instead of blowing other kids fresh sh..." She choked back the end of that. Close one. She knows I dis-like using cuss words in the house so having this on her mind she was able to stop herself. I looked curiously at her then preached "Now that was a little rough. You know she can't afford even as much as we have. She has it worse off then us. Have you looked at this through her eyes? Perhaps she acts the way she does because she can't express anything other than hate to make people know how she feels." It even didn't sound too good to me but at least I could see a bit of sympathy in Lilly's eyes.

"I guess..." She glanced over at the clock and squealed, "Oh my god! It's already four! Madison will be here in ten minutes! I haven't even found that really nice smelling spray yet! I've got to get ready!" She darted from my room leaving me in a dumbstruck state. "...Oooohhhkkkaaaayyyy...?"

I continued putting back all my things when I finally remembered my package. I sat on the edge of the bed and grasped my pocket knife from the table and flicked it open. I tried cutting slowly to build anticipation. Forget that. My knife was flying wildly around; slicing up the brown wrapped box like it was a fresh caught fish getting flayed. Before I knew it, a medium sized white box with one line on the front of it slid out from the wreckage. "May god be with you." I popped open the top of the box, tipped it over holding my hand out. Out fell a shower of Styrofoam rain and a four inch tall silver Jesus statue with a very Jesus pose.

Why would I buy something like this? I think any explanation would suffice but here is the main one. I was looking around on the internet of things that help depression. Between the many Tumblr pages and anti-depressants I stumbled upon a blog by some apparently well-known blogger asking the same question I was. In the blog, it had a poll of what things cheer depressed people up the most. Option 1 - Pills/Drugs, 13 votes, Option 2 - Cutting, 7 votes, Option 3 - Distractants/Games/Music, 9 votes, Option 4 - Social Interactions, 14 votes, Option - 5, Religion, 56 votes. I read all of the options and results over and over. All of these things didn't seem too attractive, especially since some I've tried. But my eyes got fixated on religion. It never crossed my mind that religion could alter ones mental status. Well, it probably had but I probably just didn't care. So I began looking into a religion that suited me. I eventually settled upon Christianity. Seemed the most soothing and the easiest one to follow. Go to church. Help out, don't sin, and you'll win a five star pass to happiness and afterlifeness. It's been a year since I officially joined the religion. So I wanted to show pride in what I believed in by getting something as solid and pure as I was. A silver Jesus. Right? Pure, righteous, and shiny. All good things! It's not 100% pure silver, which is kind of ironic, I could never afford something like that. Instead I got a silver plated iron statue version which was still expensive but in my price range. I was told that this statue would also help me relax and feel one with god, so I got it.

I gave it a quick wipe of some Windex to clean him up before putting him on the table next to my bed. For a minute or two I just sat there and admired it. Felt so right, ya' know? It took me a few seconds to realize that Lilly was standing once again at her spot in the door jamb just looking at me.

"I didn't know you were religious. Since when have you been a Jesus guy?" She wondered out loud, curiosity simply drowning her eyes.

"About a year now. Heard this helps your mental state or something. Kind of like Zen." Again, I didn't know if I fully believed myself.

"Hm. Oh, I got to go!" She started to run out when I lassoed her with my words. "Oi?! Kiss and hug?! Really now?!"

A groan echoed throughout the apartment and I heard her footsteps as she came bounding back in the room like a flash flood. "Hug." She basically tackled me. Guess that's what a hug is these days. "Kiss." I gave her a kiss on the forehead and simply couldn't get out of that room fast enough.

"Bye dad! Love you!" she yelled as the door slammed shut. I couldn't even register that she said that let alone reply before she was out that door.

I turned back to my statue and stared at it for a minute or two before finally blinking a few times and realizing how tired I really was. It was a long day of nonetheless. I got up, slowly due to the magnet of sleep imbedded in my bed and made my way to the kitchen to make a quick snack before I was off to bed. I had work to go to in the morning anyway. I pulled the sheets off my bed and placed me in their place and them on top of me and before switching off the bedside light, I gave that statue one last look. It just looked so right on that spot on my table. I flicked the switch off and laid there and let sleep's comforting form engulf my mind as I drifted off. I was relieved that I didn't have to stay up late to let Lilly back inside when she got home. I had her a key made recently meaning she'd be fine. And tomorrow I would awake to her sweet face with a hot cup of coffee at the ready. With really the only thing to worry about tomorrow being work, which is generally little to worry about, I drifted out of consciousness. Maybe I'm getting my life back on track.

Chapter 1: An Almost Regular Day

A beam of light coming from down the hall greeted my face and I awoke to find Lilly walking into my room. "Good morning!" She piped as she bounced into my room. She immediately shoved a cup of warm coffee in my hand and tried to drag me out of bed. It seemed like I was in slow motion and everything else was moving at twice the speed. Though, it's usually like that in my early morning delirium. While rubbing the last bits of sleep from my eyes, I got up and stretched. I caught a glimpse of the small savior in the corner of my eye. Surprisingly, it brought a smile to my face.

"Maybe this was a good idea. I might even be able to take on the day. Maybe," I thought. I recited a quick prayer that I had picked up and began my early day routine. I haphazardly threw on some old blue jeans and a fresh, bland company polo shirt provided by my work. I grabbed my half-drunk cup of coffee and headed out of my room to the dining area and took my accustomed seat at the far end of the table. As I let out a sigh, Lilly takes the seat directly across from me.

"Heeellloooo? Wake up sleepy head! Time to get ready for yet another day!" She spoke with such enthusiasm is was almost nauseating. I grumble back as a rebuttal.

"I don't wanna… just let me sleep for five more minutes…" I lay my head down on the table and moan out of tiredness. I could hear her physically frown and walk over to me and gave me a good old-fashioned shake-awake.

"Wake up! Wake up! Wake uuuupppppp!" She whined as I was jostled free of my peaceful rest and now flailing around without my control. I finally shook her off. "Alright! Alright! I'm awake! Quit ya' little bugger!" Proclaiming with a little pinch of fun in my remark. She sat back down with a smile on her face and took a bite of her bagel she had made.

"Soooo... What ya got planned for today mister? Anything exciting? Or maybe some more BS you usually put up with," she spoke as she swallowed a mouthful of bagel. She looked across at me, waiting for a response.

"Probably the same crap but you know something? I feel good. Today feels like it's going to be a good day. I can feel it. Not even measuring a whole backyard down to the smallest centimeter could shoot me out of cloud nine, well maybe 8, today," I lift my head and say with pride.

"Why's that?" she questioned, still devouring her cinnamon bagel.

I pondered this for a moment or too, making absolutely sure that I was in a better light today and how to phrase it. "Well... um... You know that new statue I got yesterday?"

"Yeah."

"Well, I don't know what exactly, but that statue just gives me more energy. I feel... invigorated when I look at it and when I did today, I felt a kind of comfort." Listening to myself, I sounded like some kind of prophet. Lilly seemed to use the same mental judgment. Following up that expression with,

"What? Pfft I've never heard you talk like that. You must have had an epiphany! What is the new discovery you've made lately, professor?" Ha. So called it. I sat there, again thinking of how to put the words together in my mouth in a way that didn't make me sound philosophical. Once I finally found the words I state plainly, "I think I've found my way to get through every single day. Between Music and god I've found a sort of eternal peace. But, only one thing has gotten me through every day to see the end then anticipate the next day."

"What's that?" she question, finally finishing her bagel and now eager to hear the main point of her father's sudden realization session.

After a good breath, I turned and looked at her, love in my eyes. "You. You made every day possible for me. Every day I wake up to you with your bright smile and sparkling eyes and I feel like I'm the luckiest man alive."

She gave that perfect trademark smile of her and came over to me "Awww. Come here," and gave me a warm hug. "I love you."

"I love you too." I spoke quietly back to her. Glancing over her shoulder I realize what time it is. I leaned into her ear and say, "Does your class start at 7:20 or 8:20?"

She paused a moment, thinking about what was said and reply, "7:20…Why?"

"Well that means class starts in 15 minutes." She immediately broke free of the heartfelt hug remembering she has school to get to. She darted down the hall and after some rustling returned quickly with a jacket on and a backpack swung over her shoulder.

"I got to go! Bye dad, love you!" and with that she was gone out the door with a rush of cool air from outside rushing in as she slammed the door shut.

Now I'm left with just me and my thoughts. I only had about an hour to finish getting ready and go. I decided to sit down and watch the morning news to see how the weather was going to be for my trek around town. I slumped down into the couch and groped around on the table till I found a controller that was familiar. Found it. I click the power and was dulled out to the TV and its staticy voices. Before I knew it, it was ten minutes before I myself had to leave so I got my jacket and swiped my keys from the holder. Not five feet from the door something hit me. A sudden urge. I left the living room and headed back into my bedroom. There it sat.

The tiny, shiny Jesus was sitting there peacefully resting on my bedside table. It seemed to speak to me and wish me to have a good day. I silently thanked the small savior with another prayer. After that I left my house, being sure to lock it, as always. I spot my little Toyota sitting there almost pleading with me to go somewhere with it. The key gently unlocked its door and I slid inside, being sure to pull my jacket all the way as to not get it caught on a tooth of the vicious door. Another key was used to rev the engine to life. The gears in the transmission growled and sputtered as I pulled out of my parking spot and rolled away to my monotonous job.

The day seemed to ease by. A simple day, not too complicated. Just the normal business trying to get permission to buy an industrial sized dumpster for behind the business and the couple people trying to get a permit to build a pool somewhere on the property. Which don't you think is a little odd? I mean, a brand spanking new pool right before winter, in one of the coldest fall months. Pssh. Not my cash. So oh well.

That was pretty simple enough and with a rock album I got about a month ago and never listened to, bumping through my ear buds the day went by relatively quick.

I got home a little later than usual; striking up a conversation with a hot gas station employee tends to kill a bit of time. I rolled up and put the car to park. Walking up to the door I tried to open it, as usual Lilly would be home by now and tends to leave the door unlocked, a found myself walking straight into the door with my nose smacking hard against the solid oak. Locked? Hmm, a little weird. I pulled my keys from my pocket and unlocked the door to find the house was dead silent. That kind of eerie silence that usually transpires when a small crowd of people are all chatting and suddenly go deathly silent. It was almost deafening.

"Lilly? You home?" I yelled throughout the room as a shut the door behind me. I was still greeted to that same silence. Maybe Lilly just isn't home yet. Did she say something about staying after today? I don't think so. But still, it didn't bother me too bad as opened my bedroom door and began emptying my pockets. I was just about to take my shoes off when I realized something. I saw that the place normally reserved for my Jesus was empty. I didn't move it, did I? I walked around the house and even checked Lilly's room. Nothing. What the hell? Why would it be gone? At this I began to get frustrated. The anger of having a wonderful day and coming home to this crap made me blurt out.

"Where the hell is my tiny Jesus!" Not a moment after, I heard the door shut and a quiet and calm coo came drifting down the hall.

"Dad? Hello?" I came back out from checking in the kitchen to see Lilly standing there, adorned in her usual black and pink jacket and skirt with a face that simply leaked questions. "What was that all about?" She had apparently heard the end of my little rant and burst of anger.

"Oh hey." I said. "Sorry about that. I seemed to have misplaced my silver Jesus guy that I got yesterday. Lilly still had a looked of bewilderment but look around the room for no more than a second or two and pointed over to my CD collection in the corner of the living room. "Isn't that it over there?"

I turned my head over to that area and, who would have guessed, it was sitting there on the top of the stacks of CDs simply staring out at us like we were stupid for not noticing it earlier. I leap at the stand and snatched the statue from its perch. Glancing down at him I can't get rid of this dumbfounded look on my face. Why was it out here? Did I move it without remembering? "Lilly, did you move this statue from my room?" I ask half hoping for a reasonable explanation.

"Nope. You've seen me leave the house and come back. I haven't been home yet." She replied simply.

"Ok." I look back down at the statue and then back at Lilly, a newfound question on my mind. "Well why are you late home?"

"Oh. I went to Madison's for a bit to hang and do some homework. Sorry about that." A half guilty pose became apparent on her.

I sigh. "Yea that's ok. You sure you didn't move this though?"

"Positive." She turned and disappeared into her room.

This didn't comfort me at all. Why was it here? The thought left me feeling quite unsafe. I guess I can't let this

get to me. I have bigger things to worry about. I have to wait for a phone call from Jessica, my lawyer. She's calling to give me a status on my current situation in the custody battle. Hm. My pocket is vibrating. I pull out my phone and, speak of the devil, Jessica is calling. I step out onto the back porch; well more or less a five by five foot fenced in cube. Basically my office. Half an hour later, sure as shit, she called to tell me Janice is pushing harder on child support and trying to get more days. Freaking crazy chick. Jessica told me that she had things together but she's holding on by a thread. One slip up and I'd be screwed. I reassured that I had it under control and hung up. I came inside and spotted my little guy sitting on the stack again. I left it on the chair where I put it down to answer my phone. I grabbed it walked quickly to my room and placed it back the spot it should go. That's twice now. I went over to Lilly's door and pushed open. She was sitting on her bed unpacking her things from her bag. When I asked her if she came out of her room when I was outside, she only said,

"Um. No? I've been sitting in here relaxing since I came home."

Chapter 2: House Call For Father Wilkes

The next two weeks went off without a hitch. Same calming mind set. Lilly has been doing fine. Janice hasn't given me any fresh shit for anything which is always good and just as relieving; the statue hasn't done any unwarranted traveling. Things are going pretty well. Today is my birthday and from the moment I woke up, I felt like this was going to be one of the best days I've had in a long time. The usual morning routine went just as usual as they come. Lilly didn't remember it was my birthday but then again, what kid does know their parents day of birth? Not many. I came into the office and went to my station to see what today's tasks are. I fall into my beat up old rolly chair and grab my assignment sheet. Let's see. An elderly woman needs permission to have a pre-paid for renovation of her bathroom and the piping to be reworked. A fair task. Next on the list, the local bar, Jims' Eat Em' and Beat Em', needs new lighting which calls for a replacing of all the wires in the whole damn place for the whacky fist shaped lights. I hate bartenders. That'll take most the day. And the last two...blah blah blah. Maybe I can have one of my co-workers whose list isn't too filled up take up those. After all, it is my birthday so why not? I'd do it for someone else, so why not me? I left the building and put my buds in as I got into my tin can car and speeded off to a day's work.

As I thought, the day went just about how I thought it would. The elderly woman's bathroom wasn't the cleanest but better than some I've seen. I gave her an estimate and said I would be back in a few days to check up on her and the installing crew. The bar was tougher than I thought. They had closed the place for the day just for me. How sweet. Well apparently the owner got bored waiting for me and decided to get hammered. So I dealt with a drunken old soak following me around while I did my job, not bothering to talk to him much at, for around five hours. After that tiring ordeal I made my way back to the office to relax for the rest of the day. Reluctantly, a friend of mine took my other tasks as I remember he also owed me a favor. Last year around this time, he got wasted at a bar across town and didn't have a ride and no one else would come and get his sorry ass so I kind of had no choice. Still, he was happy to take the other two tasks and wish me a happy birthday before heading off for the rest of the day. So I sat in the lounge area for the better part of the day. I watched the hours tick past and zoned out a few times getting woken up by the occasional employee getting a bite to eat or some coffee.

The clock finally hit two and it was time to finally head out of here. A grabbed my jacket sitting on the chair next to me. Just as I was leaving the room, I was greeted with a blob of sweat and a smell of old shaving cream. My boss, Mr. Chuck Warburton looked more surprised than me.

"Sorry about that." I say and try and squeeze past him but he was clearly blocking me in.

"Not actually, I'm glad I found someone. We got a call recently and no one is here to take it. Which leaves..."

"Where is everyone else?" I rudely cut him off. May have been a little mean but I couldn't care less.

He choked back his old statement and made a new one like that. "They're all out, you can take this one." The smell of alcohol permeating the air. You also could most likely cut that stupid eager tone of his when he gets to ruin someone's plans for the day with a butter knife. He handed me a clip board with the papers stuck to it.

"Really? I mean my shift ended about, oh, ten minutes ago and its my birthday, so if you would." I tried once more to move past him but that globe shaped form of his was taking up the entire doorway.

"Is that right? Well, too bad. You don't see anyone else complaining when I have them stay a little extra. I like to think they like their jobs, so they do it anyway. So why not be a team player and take it on faith." He shoved the clipboard into my hands and gave his pig-like smile. He pushed me aside and waddled his way over to the vending machine. I was frozen were my foot stood. What a five star asshole! I nearly broke that stupid clipboard. People wouldn't take any crap from you if you didn't have the power to really screw us over. Just wait till someone knocks you down a peg. I'd love to see his face when the CEO of this company comes up here and breaks the news that his porky ass is now jobless and the company shuts down. Oh what a sweet retard for putting up with his crap. Maybe I stay here for the job, but I think a better reason I stay is just to be there the day he gets what's coming to him. That'd be a wonderful day. If only that day was today. That'd make it perfect.

Whatever. I took my clipboard and got into my car for one last trip. I started to look at where my destination was and realized it was at the only church in town. They needed to have the pipes redone since the rust on them as finally worn through and is now leaking in the walls and basement. Seeing this made me smile a little bit. Not sure why. Maybe the idea of being on a holy place on the day of my birth was somehow comforting. I made my way across town and pulled into the parking lot and the engine whirled to a stop. I was walking up and thought for a minute. I shouldn't listen to my music player while I was here. Disrespectful. I pulled my buds and turn the shuffler to stand by. Shoving into my pocket I made my way up and into the doors. I was met by an empty chapel with not even the soul of god present, it felt like. Something felt missing. I've been here before. I relatively small church, it's been here for around 230 years and is, needless to say, in need of desperate work. Originally, the colors were a vibrant tan on the walls, white ceiling, real stained oak trim around the floors and doors, and a dark stone floor but has since become faded and tarnished. The roof was old and moldy, wallpaper is peeling off in random spots, and the old stone tiles are cracked and filled with dirt. I felt bad that the city didn't pay for the place to get redone. That's kind of like slapping the big man in white in the face.

"Hello? Who comes in?" A voice came from behind me. I turned to see an older man, white beard and too many wrinkles to count in a traditional pastors get up coming up from a stairwell, I assume to the basement. He kind of startled me simply for the fact that if you see a ghost, white as a sheet, appearing behind you would give any regular man a jump.

"Oh yea. Hi. My name is Andrew. I'm from that zoning company that needs to talk to about your pipes." I extended my hand as per usual in any house call. He lit up and clasped me hand with both of his.

"Ah yes. Praise god they heard me. Thank you so much for your time. Please, follow me." He said. Even his voice was rittled of age, filled with bumps and wheezes. He started to make his way down the stairs once more. I adjusted my papers around to get the page I use to write down the status on to the top of my little stack. Soon after I followed him to the basement.

Surprisingly enough, the basement was rather well kept. Boxes and other rugs and such neatly stacked in organized piles. Carpeted. Nice plastered walls and great lighting. The only things setting the whole atmosphere off was a water worn wall on the far wall and a musky smell floating around aimlessly. In a corner I could see another stairway that split off in two directions. I can only guess that one went to the stage and pedestal in the main hall and the other heading into the office and room of the pastor himself.

"Alrighty what have you got for me today mister..."

He was busy moving things around so that I could reach the far wall. "Me? Father Wilkes. First name Elijah. Just call me father."

"Will do father. What have you got for me today?" I come over and start helping him move things around.

"These confounded pipes have finally breathed their last breath. They began to leak around a couple days ago."

"What were these pipes made of? Aluminum or iron?"

"Oh...I'm not quite sure. I'm pretty sure iron."

"How long have they been in the building?"

"Oh...Let me think...Around six-...no, seventy years ago. Around the time we bought the place."

I almost dropped a box I was moving. "Seventy years?! And they only went bad now? That incredible! Normal true iron pipes like these rust in about ten to thirty years." He didn't seem so impressed.

"Yes well. My family put these in after we bought the place and they haven't gone bad since about the time I took over a year ago when my father passed away."

"Hm well I wouldn't if they gave out any day now. Good thing we're going to fix it now and not having that water leaking do permanent damage to the rest of the building such as mold or wood rot." We finally finished moving all the random crap around and I was able to reach the wall. "You mind if I break open a little bit of wall to see what really is going on?"

"Not at all. Go right ahead. If you don't mind, I need to excuse myself. I was tending to other business before you came and I must really get back to it."

"Will do father." And with that he was up the second set of stairs. From below I heard his door shut.

I reached into my pocket and pulled out my pocket knife and flicked it open. I then proceeded to cut into the water soaked part of the wall. After some time I was able to break through the plaster and see inside. Perfect choice of wall to deface. Right above the pipe. Sure enough, the old pipe was rusted as all get out. The water which was coming out was a murky brown and it all smelled musky. Found the source of the odor. Yup. That's iron piping, and what do you know? It's really freaking old. He wasn't joking around. Yup this guy needs this renovation. I filled out my end of the necessary paperwork and with a successful click of my pen; I came out from the jumble of boxes and random gadgets. I made my way up the stairs and up to what I presumed to be the father's room. Knock knock. "Father? You in there?" No answer. I opened the door slowly, cautiously and as quietly as possible. I peek inside. I'm dumb. Broom closet. From my left I hear a whistle. The pastor came out of his room and made his way over to me.

"What did you find down there?" He asked.

"Not much. Just a paper showing clearance to get new pipes and a rework of some the walls."

"Great to hear! Praise god! Thank you so much kind sir! Here, for your troubles. I found these at the market and they looked so good. I doubt I'll every eat them and they're too good to waste." He handed me a Shiny bag of marmalade candies, with a note attached saying "May god be with you."

"Thank you very much father. I would stay and chat, you seem like an ok guy, but I really must get back to my daughter. I'm not so sure she has her key with her today and I very much doubt she'd be able to get in through locked windows.

"Oh! Then by no means let me keep you. Please, go to her. In any case, I believe our paths will cross again." He proclaimed while ushering me out the door.

"Yes, that can be arranged. I'll need to come by later when the plumbing crew arrives to give them the proper paperwork and clearance and such. Don't worry too much. God has his ways. I'm sure we'll meet again." I say walking awayfrom him.

"A man of god are you?" His words stopped me in my tracks for a moment. I turned on my heels to face him.

"Why of course. For a while now. He's been very supportive in my hard times."

"Ah so that's why."

"Why what?"

"You carry it."

This puzzled me. "Carry what, if I may ask."

He gestured to my jacket pocket. "The son of our lord."

I froze. Looking down I see a hint of silver poking out from my pocket. Without really feeling anything, I reach numbly down and pluck the tiny statue from my pocket. I stare the miniature man in the eyes as he stares back. What is this...doing in my pocket...This doesn't make...sense...I feel the old man now uncomfortably close now. I hadn't seen him even move.

"Ah and might I say, what a nice touch of silver."

"Um...Yea...I...I d-don't..." I stammered. What is this? Is this really my statue or something of my mind? What the hell is happening?

"Hm, my father had one like that once. Oh my my! Look at the time! You must be so late home to your daughter! Please you must be on your way." Now pushing me out the front door and I land with my feet barely a couple steps below.

"Um yes well...I'll see you...Uh in a f-few days... Uh ok?" My mind still numb from the recent events, my eyes held firmly on the little man.

"Oh absolutely! Oh and Andrew?" He says as he stands in the doorway.

"Things aren't always what they seem to be..." My eyes snap from the statue to the old man now. Our eyes locked in

an intense gaze. What? I thought to myself. "...Oh, and s
to Lilly for me if you would. She's such a nice girl." He now
closed the door and locked it behind him.

Chapter 3: The Precious Gift Of Silver

I amble to my car and get inside and shut the door. I just sit there in the quiet of the car. The last of his words

barely registering in my mind. Who was this guy? Who the hell did he think he was? What the hell is my statue doing on my person? What the hell is going on? I look back into my hand at the tiny man and all he does is stare back. Like moving around without physically being moved the most normal thing in the world to him and it was ok to shatter someone's reality like such. I hardly felt me turn the key or me driving away from the freaking church. Time simply didn't apply to me as before I knew it I was sitting in my parking spot in Crystal Heights Apartments. I turned the car off and grabbed hold of my keys, my tiny savior and made my way to my front door. When I'm inside, I slump into the couch and just sit there. I'm just sitting there. What just happened not twenty minutes ago...I don't even kn-

The whine of the squeaky front door yells out and in comes Lilly with her normal bag and a small black gift bag. "Happy B-day dad!" She squeals as she comes bounding over to me and locks me in a warm embrace. She pulls back, her arms on my shoulders and looks into my face. Her happy smile quickly fades into concern as she asks, "What's wrong? You should be happy!"

I glance down at my hand in which the tiny man was in. He wasn't there. Just a shiny bag of marmalade candy.

"...What...the...?" I say but am cut off by Lilly's curiosity.

"Ooo! You got a gift from someone! Who'd you get it from?" She got up and sat next to me, grabbed the bag from my hand and started to examine it thoroughly.

I quickly throw a glance to my music stack. Nothing. I get up and almost run to my room. As glance down at my table by the bed. My silver man is just sitting there. Staring at nothing in particular. Just resting on its platform of a bottom, all cozy and peaceful. I pick him up and gaze into its heartless eyes and he does the same. What is that? After a moment or two of powerful squinting, I notice a small chip, under the chin, where the regular silver is showing off that dull iron underneath with a small bit of rust forming at the center of the blemish. Did I do that? I put him down and left the room. Coming back into the living room I'm met with a concerned looking Lilly in my face with the bag of candy still in her hand. I just sigh and go into the kitchen. I need something to calm me down. I grab some Lays and a cold Budweiser. I don't drink. It's just relaxing. Least not a heavy drinker. I crack it open on my teeth. I need music. I throw on some Beethoven and play it through my stereo. Finally I come to a rest on the couch, chips and beer in hand. Moments later Lilly joins me.

"Are you ok?" She grabs my hand with a chip midair to my mouth. Those sparkling sky blue eyes staring at me with a feeling of legitimate worry flowing from them, not in tears, in unspoken words.

"Yea...Just a long day." I reassure her and close my eyes for a minute or too.

Could all that just happen really be real? Did that all really happen? Maybe it was just a dream? It was all so real though. Time felt real. All my senses felt too real for just a dream. Perhaps I'm too stressed out. I've heard others talk about how much I've been through and still going through and how rough it has to be. Maybe I just got tired and passed out in the lounge room and didn't really feel myself drive home. Maybe I stopped in the local market and bought those candies. The length of time I was doing "overtime" was well pass the time Lilly gets home from school and so a dream, stressed induced or not, would explain why I still got here before her like usual. Yea. That makes sense. I'm just over reacting. Nothing happened during that time. Just my trusty old mind messing with me. Ha-ha! Maybe that's its way of saying, "Happy thirty third birthday Andrew!" Yup. Just my imagination.

I open my eyes a few minutes later to find Lilly still waiting for a response that doesn't suck. I give her a real smile of relief and give her a hug and say "Yea I'm fine. C'mere you!" We roll around on the couch laughing.

Afterwards we sat back normal and after a good breath she said, "Ah, so glad your ok. For a minute you looked legitly...something..."

"Yup. I'm alright." I remember the black gift bag and look for it. After spotting it I look at her and ask, "What's in the bag?"

As if remembering the bag herself her expression lit up, a smile practically going ear to ear, spread across her face and she leaned over and retrieved the small plastic bag. She holds it in front of her face, covering her mouth with it as she says, "I got you something...Ya' know. It's your birthday." Every word coated in excitement. She then holds out the small bag and waits for me to grab it. I snatch the little bag from her.

"I know how much you love music..." She goes on as I begin to open it.

"...and I know how you love religion and god..." I hesitate, only for a moment or two then remembering that that was all just a dream and that I'm just a silly "old" man and continue unwrapping it.

"...so I paid my friend with my money to use his parents credit card to go and buy this off I site I found." This time I do stop. I cast her a disapproving glance as any good parent should do in a situation like this. She shrugs and says, "Calm down. You'll love it."

After a few more seconds of pause I give up and continue unwrapping until the small square is revealed. I salvage it from the wreckage of the wrapping paper and tape. It's a CD. I speak the album and band out loud, the name so strange. I never heard of them but I'm sort of drawn to this CD. Why? I don't know. It calls to me. I make sure to say it properly to unsure I fully understand the name. I can't help but notice a coincidence that makes my heart sink a few feet.

"Carved In Stone album by Messiah of Silver..."

"Yup! They're some band I found while surfing the high seas of the interwebs and found it on eBay. I typed in religious music but most of it looked pretty gospel and chorusy. I instead searched religious band. On around the fifth page, there was an older looking CD case and cover but the description was pretty convincing. So, I bought it!" She looked at me with great anticipation for the answer to the next question. "Do you like it?"

I'm still sitting there staring at this old beaten up case and read the song names one by one:

1. -Rust on the Hammer- Hm, seems like a rock song or something.

2. -Take Me Away- An upbeat traveling song?

3. -Silver in my Wrists- Charming...

4. -Lift Me High- Now that sounds like a religious song.

5. -Hold Me Down- Ehh. Violent or suggestive much? Who knows.

6. -Nails of Silver- Hm, this band must have like silver or something.

7. -Tear Stained Cross- Sounds sad or depressing.

All and all it seemed odd but still I might like this band. The case itself has the two commandment stones next to each, seeming to depict god handing them to Jesus with a glorious light bathing him. Like I said, the case is old and dusty so much of the color has faded. The back of the case showed the song names in order with the same picture behind the words. I open the case and look at the CD itself. It's shiny in a swirly pattern etched on it. I pop the CD from its holder and look at the back of it. Wow, that's surprising. Not a single mark or scratch. All I can see is my reflection peering back at my curiously as well as little tiny particles of dust beginning to stick to the seemingly new CD. I put it back into its case and close it. I can feel Lilly's eager eyes still waiting for my lips to say the words she wants to hear.

"I love it." I gave my best smile, "Thank you so much."

She lit up and flung to me and gave me another hug. "Happy birthday."

Looking over her shoulder I spot the clock and say, "So you want to eat here in about an hour?"

"Mk. I'll go do my assignments for a bit. Just gemme' a call when you want to eat." Proud with pleasing her father with the dusty CD, she trotted back into her room and shut the door. Soon after I heard her own music begin to bump.

Well that was still nice. Giving one last look at the CD, I stood and placed it on my stack. I'll listen to it over the weekend. I come back over to the couch and grab my pile of trash and wrappings and throw them away. I lay down onto the couch once more and finished of my beer and polished off more than half of the chips. Satisfied with a good, but strange day so far, I lay and slowly nod off for the better part of that hour. Snapping back awake, I call Lilly to let her know dinner was going to start being made. I eventually got up and with the help of Lilly, we made spaghetti from scratch. We both loved to home cook. We didn't eat out much. A fast food place's food is pretty nasty after eating it for so long. We ate at the table for once in a while and chatted on and on about her past and funny as well as embarrassing stories from my past. We killed and hour and a half without relishing it. I put the dishes away while Lilly cleaned off the table. We sat and chatted in the living room for another hour. Before either of us knew it, it was 9:30 and the nighttime routine had to begin. I went and hopped in the shower while she cleaned up around the house a bit. After I got out, I went into my room. I sat on my bed, towel wrapped around my waist. I give a sigh and glance over to the Jesus statue whose seems to be staring at me. "Pervert." I say at him. "Ggiiiirrrlll you know wanna peak. Well heeellll nooo. You gota' put a ring on it first baaabaaayy."

Whoa. To much of me falling asleep in front of the TV when a late night show showing some cocky black chicks has got be doing it too. Still funny has hell. I hear Lilly coming down the hall.

"Hey dad, you save me any hot water? You in he-" She says as she comes in my room and immediately turns back out. "Oh my god dad. Put some clothes on for Christ's sake. Just because it's your birthday doesn't mean that you are allowed to parade around the house in your birthday suit. Geez!" She left and went to get in the shower.

I shut my door and let the towel fall as I go to my dresser to grab any form of comfortable garb or cloak that suits me. Long johns. Good enough. I slip them on and lay down into my bed. I switch the light out and let the darkness grab at me from all sides. I lay there thinking of what my day tomorrow will consist of. Well, I got to get up early enough to wake Lilly and have her get ready to leave. Tomorrow and Sunday is Janice's days. It sucks to not see Lilly those two days but I count myself pretty lucky since even though Janice has primary custody, she gladly gave me the weeks while she kept the weekends. I don't know if it's she doesn't want Lilly to switch schools and move away from her friends or if it's the idea that she knows she'll win this whole thing and will have Lilly permanently soon enough. Stuck up crazy ass bitch...May be rude and cowardly to talk about someone behind their back but sometimes it's just too hard to hold back your anger. I open my eyes and give one last glance over to my statue and pray to him good night. My eyes drooping with sleep I rolled back, now unable to fight against the weight in my eyelids anymore, I let sleep take me and I feel into a deep sleep.

Chapter 4: "Aw, Come On Jesus. Five More Minutes..."

I woke in the middle of the night, covered in sweat with my blanket wrapped around my legs and gave a good amount of rustling around, accidentally hitting my arm against the wall fairly hard. I sat straight up in my bed and took well needed deep breaths. That was awful... My night terror tantrum seemed to make Lilly stir a bit. I could hear her down the hall rustling around in her bed tiring to get comfy again. Both of our doors were open so just about any noise made by either of us traveled a long way. I sat there and tried to gather my bearing. I stand and walk over to the light switch, flicking it on, while still remembering to close my door as to not wake her again. I sat back down on the corner of my bed and rested my head in my hands. Freaking dreams man. But something about this one was...different.

Usually, in the past few months I've had dreams about normal stuff for me. My mind telling me what my situation was and what to do next, using weird and crazy physical metaphors and representations to show them. Normally such as me driving Lilly around. Nowhere in particular and running low on gas. I took it that as me running into a wall in my custody battle and not knowing what to do. Soon though, I found a gas station and wouldn't you know it, Jessica came up and pumped my gas. Maybe saying she's my only way to keep going and stay strong. But the ones lately have been even more strange. About two weeks ago...Come to think of it, that's around the time I had got my statue...Anyway. I saw myself getting horribly murdered or mugged when on my usual job runs.

One recently was me going into an abandoned building and seeing a shady figure walk at me from behind a wall and I couldn't get back out the door. He would run at me and tackle me to the ground and pull a long sickle from his coat. He would laugh and cut my shirt open. He would be sitting on my stomach, knees pinning my arms down to the ground. He brought the sickle to my chest and carved a sentence I couldn't quite read at my position. The pain would be excruciating and numbing at the same time. I would then appear over my body, probably from the eyes of the killer, seeing me struggle and writhe in pain. The sentence on my chest became, at that moment clear. It read "NO MAN OR WOMAN ESCAPES THE WRATH OF GOD." The pain would be still surging through me and at that point my body convulsed one last time as he hooked the sickle through the bottom of my jaw and have it stick back out of my mouth. A scream would ring through the air, I think it was probably Lilly's and I would wake to my status that I have tonight.

Another one is of me. But I'm not me. Not really. I'm in Janice's body sitting comfortably on one of her many fancy couches watching some stupid show. From behind I would feel a hand grab my mouth and another around my neck as I was pulled from the couch. I then be dragged through my house and thrown onto my kitchen table. It didn't matter how hard I struggled. I couldn't stop this man. He then proceeded to get onto the table and undo his pants. After I was raped he would grab some nails from his pocket. Now that I think about it, I think it was the same man as before. He pulled a hammer from another pocket and nailed me crudely to the table. Two nails through both of my wrists and ankles. As was before, the pain too intense to even register. My screams rested on deaf ears and soon went flat with a nail through the throat. He stopped to shut the fuck up. He pulled the same bloodied sickle from his pocket and rip my shirt open to begin carving some more. This time that I went into his eyes the line he was writing so intricately on my exposed chest read, "THE LUST FOR PENANCE IS BITTER SWEET AND ALSO A FALSE COURSE." I then passes out and saw my body, maybe a few hours later, bleeding all over the table and onto the floor. Instantly I was face to face with a terror stricken face of Janice with that same scream drowning out all other sounds.

Today was different, much different. I'm sitting at my little cubicle at my office. No one else seemed to be there at the time. I'm doing some sort of filing or paperwork when I just stop in the middle of it all. And I sat there. Just sitting there. Something made me glance to my right of my desk and see little Jesus standing there in all his pride. His head seemed to look up a little at me. We just sit there and stare at each other. His features seemed to physically loosen up. His face then went completely loose, similar to a human and told me in plain, simple, language, "He who desires penance, sins to do so. That which seems right is false. Only god's judgment rules over man. You've wronged me Andrew. You've spit at the feet of god. Why would you do this? He is displeased. He demands obedience. No man is above him. Now pray. Pray upon the deaf ears of your former father. Pray. Prayer is needed. For penance. No... You're past penance. Pray. Pray with all your might...

Pray...

For...

MERCY."

Blood began to trickle then pour from the center of his chest. The bleeding refused to stop flowing. My mouth felt like it was being pulled open wide. The rest of me is frozen to the spot. The blood now covering my entire desk and falling on the floor, splattering against my feet. With my mouth fully open to its max and then some, my mind races. It can't seem to focus on any one thing. The statues mouth began to go slack jawed, stretching down far past what is physically possible by any human. As he did this a low guttural, demonic tone took place of the saviors and warned in a volume so loud my ears felt like they were bleeding.

"Pray for your soul. Not to me. To god. He won't save you however. For he has lost faith for you. Still, pray for mercy. Now to me. Maybe you could stir some mercy up from deep within my form."

With his last word spoken, he let out a monstrous, low, growl. His face seemed to twist into one of horror. He started to shake and vibrate in the table, first slowly then more and more violently. Now with blood flying in every direction it was hard to see him fly from the table into my elongated mouth down my throat. My mouth snapped shut soon after and I fell to the ground wheezing and gasping for air, the tiny man cutting off my airflow through my windpipe. It began to burn. Stinging and singeing my trachea, my mind began to shatter. I fell through the floor. Then another. As if I was on a thirty story high building. Once I reached the bottom floor I felt and heard, felt more than heard, the sickening cracks ripple throughout my body as I hit the concrete floor. After I hit, I woke violently.

All of it was just so violent and vivid. Just the realism of the dream sent me into paranoia and insecurity. I sat there on the corner of the bed in the dim light for the better part of a couple hours. I had to go back to sleep. I needed it. I had to get up early. I couldn't afford to be tired. I got up and turned the light back off reintroducing me to the darkness. I laid down and pulled the drenched covers back over my body. I turned to look at that damn statue in the readjusted lighting. He just sat there, dull expression, right hand down and left hand to his chest. Fuck looking at you...rolling on my side I was drifting slowly back to sleep when a noise ruined it all for me. From about two or three feet behind me, it was so faint I had to strain to hear but at the same time crystal clear, and if it was in my mind's ear or if I really heard didn't matter, I heard the sound. It came quiet and low.

"Pray."

I didn't sleep the rest of the night.

Chapter 5: Simple Days, Unclear Waves

The sun finally poked through my curtains and hit me dead center in the face. I almost jumped at this, still being

rattled up by last night. I could hear Lilly moving about the house, most likely starting her morning routine. God my head hur-...wait no...Fuck god...Man my head hurts and my eyes burn. I lazily glance over to the clock and realize I'm a half hour behind schedule. Shit. I jolted up, rubbing the last of sleep from my still weary eyes. I hurriedly throw on some jeans and a plain old shirt. I grab the door knob and stumble out into the living room were Lilly is happily watching some cartoons on

the TV. It doesn't matter she's 14. She still looked cute looking away from the screen to give me a big smile and those cheery words coming from those pretty pink lips. "Mmmoooorrrnnninnnn' sleepy head. Finally you're up. You never wake up late on Saturday." She gazed at my crusted face and could most likely smell me from where she sat. "Wow. You don't look so good. You ok?"

"Yea. Yea. Just...didn't get much sleep last night. That's all." I tried to give a halfhearted smile but failed even at

that. Man I feel awful. Clearly she didn't buy it this time. She could see something was up.

"Um. No. Not this time. Usually lately I've just shrugged it off but you've been going downhill for a little while now. Come on. Tell me."

"It's nothing. Promise." I began to walk to the kitchen but was grabbed on the arm and pulled back. She moved quickly.

"No. Tell me." She looked generally concerned. Love showing behind her eyeliner inside her eyes. She really cares right now. Maybe I shouldn't beat around the bush like this. It might just make her mad.

"Just had a rough night. Uh, Um...." I stammered, "Uh...d-...Nightmare. I had a nightmare last night. I guess it kind of took its toll on me. Just didn't get much sleep that's all."

"Are you sure?" She said. Now she was getting pretty peevish.

"Yes, Yes. I'm alright. You ready to go yet?" I retort. This seemed to make her frown a little bit. She walked off towards the kitchen.

-sigh- "Not yet. I'm not done eating."

"Alright well hurry up. We have to leave in about an hour. Ok?" I say but she just mumbled back.

"Ok?"

"Fine!" She snapped. I don't know whether she meant those words to be that sharp but none the less they hung in the air like sharp knives dangling from the ceiling.

Did I make her made or something? Guess I came off kind of forceful but I didn't

think on it too much. Dancing around the ceiling knife stricken air, I made my way to get something to eat myself. I was hungry. Usually I felt famished after the dreams and more tired than when I fell asleep. I think it's due to the physical strain I endured in the dream. Oh! I should make that into an exercise and send it into one of those crappy daytime fitness shows for stay at home moms. When you get home, find an object and make it have super-natural properties. It will make you have nightmares since it is all you can think about. In your dreams, struggle as much as possible. When you wake, don't sleep for the rest of the night. Perfect solution to that stubborn belly fat! Lose pounds in weeks! The thought made me smile.

I got into the kitchen and made a bee line for the fridge. I opened the fridge door to only be greeted by a wave of

rancid smelling, potent poison filled air. "What the fuck?!" All my food was rotten and molded. The new food was imploded on itself and the leftovers had little white forests growing on them. The condiments turned from their original bright colors to a sour tinted green and grey. Some of the food was leaking onto the trays that supported the different tiers of food and was starting to crust.

"Lilly!? What happened to all of our food!?" I shouted which wasn't necessary since I had forgotten that she was over at the table not five feet from me. She just turned away from her Poptart and said.

"What do you want? What do you mean the food?" She clearly hadn't noticed since she had gotten her food from the cupboard and never really cooks anything fresh from the carton or wrapping such as the sausage or eggs.

"I mean all of our food is rotten! Did you leave the fridge open all night or something?" I could no longer take the smell and shut the door.

"No!" She replied. "I haven't touched the fridge since yesterday and all the food was fine. Ew that does smell awful!" The wall of scent finally hitting her.

"Well. I got to fix that now. Fine, finish eating and get ready. We'll leave in a bit." I walked away and down the hall to my room. She just turned back to her food and went on her morning.

Great, now I had to clean out my entire fridge and also buy all new food. I just went fucking shopping! Probably have to scrub out my fridge until that horrible smell is gone. Maybe I can do it when I get back. I went into my room and slumped down on my bed. Pulling my left sock on, then the right, and grabbing some random crap off my table, I can't help but notice that my statue seems to be growing a beard. Not of hair, of rust...and on his neck. I stop my current tasks and reach for him. Holding him in my hand a flip him around to see that the tiny spot of rust forming under his chin had since grown into a much bigger spot on his neck. The rust coming of in my hand it seems, denser, thicker, stranger. I'm not sure how or why but the way the metal felt against my chaliced skin seemed off. Why is he rusting? He should rust like this unless some insane voodoo Chinese water torture was being done to him in my sleep. The silver itself was pretty tough for being so thin in the first place. It would take a couple strong finger nail scrapes to get it to come off. It wasn't by any means a toy. It is a valuable figurine usually shown off at a party on the shelf or something. But I had hardly touched it and I doubt Lilly had anything to do with, for how ignorant she has been acting to all that's been happening lately.

Still puzzled I put him back on his little perch and went about my business. We finally got ready and got in my car. I pulled away from the apartment and speeded off to Janice's rendezvous. The whole idea was dumb but I agreed in court on it. Granted, I didn't like to drive 50 miles away but it sure as hell beat driving all the way to northern Montana just to drop Lilly off and drive all the way home. Me and Lilly didn't talk much on the way there. This was normal. We didn't need to speak as much as we shared silent thoughts, even though we couldn't understand each other. It's kind of like talking in a chat room with just you and one other person but both speak different tongues. It's nearly impossible to understand one another but still share the same mindset. So we sit there and let the car carry us to the location, the hum of the car and the sound of wind rushing between us and other cars being the only noise.

Around forty minutes of driving later, we finally pulled up to the desolate parking lot outside of a rather old cafe.

I turned the key off and pulled it from its slot. The light hum of the car being replaced with a numbing silence again. Our silent words still filling the air. A few minutes pass till another vehicle comes rolling into the parking area, headlights piercing the early morning dew. It's a white SUV, hardly looking a week off the lot that made my little Toyota car seem like a dirt covered rock compared to a shining bar of platinum. It came to a stop right in front of my car, maybe eight feet away from the bumper, bearing down on my piece of shit car, waiting for a small girl to immerge from inside.

"Well, I guess I got to go." she said solemnly. She started to get out of the car when I caught her with the words,

"Hey." She turned. "I love you."

"I love you too dad." She leaned back in and we embraced each other then she slid from my car. She shut the door behind her and made her way to the menacing SUV.

When she got to the door of the passenger side door she cast one last look in my direction. We caught each other's eyes and held it there for a minute. I could never imagine what I'd do if I had lost her. She seemed to think the same thing. She didn't want any of this but, it's happening. She just wanted it to be over and for her to live in one place for an extended period of time without worry about the uncertainty of the future. She only had one problem that shadowed all others. Who would she live with? She knew she couldn't live with both but yet she wanted to settle somewhere. She loved both of us too much for her to break the others heart. She's too young to make a decision like this. She shouldn't have to go through this. I don't wish the curse upon anyone. Anyone who has felt this longing and eternal pain, they have my sympathy.

The enormous white door shut and the engine roared back to life. Without a moment's hesitation, she backed out from in front of me and sped off past me to the exit marked in concrete. I just sat there and rested for a few minutes. Mostly just resting my eyes for the lack of sleep coupled with the early morning rise and the 50 mile drive I have done so far and the return trip as well. I told hold of my keys once more, putting them into the slot, and kicking my car back awake. It didn't want to and neither did I but we had to get home somehow. I followed the same route Janice took to get out of the lot and sped off in the direction of my own home. I have got so much work to do when I get home. "I don't wanna'." I pouted like a spoiled kid. My plan is to check the mail, get into something comfy, grab some trash bags, empty and clean out my refrigerator, do some laundry, clean off the dishes, vacuum, and probably some other mindless crap the someone has to do on a weekend or every other. I think while doing all this, I'll listen to the CD Lilly gave me to pass the time while the excitement of listening to something new always kept my spirits running high.

After what seemed like an eternity and then some, I finally pulled into my spot at CHA. I went over to the mailbox to check to see mostly for if Jessica had sent those papers I need. Bill, bill, bill, bill, advertisement, bill, missing child, newspaper, cigar catalogue. Nothing. "Fine." I said to myself and made my way inside. As soon as I made my way inside, I noticed that the house was empty, duh, but it had a sort of presence in the hair. The kind of feeling you get when you walk into a restaurant late at night and only one other person is there but you don't quite notice them right away, was what I was feeling when I went in and shut the door. Standing in the middle of the living room, I listened to the silence for a bit before I remembered I had things to do and headed off to my room to begin to get comfy. Remerging a few minutes later with a pair of clean long johns, the ONLY clean pair, and a wind breaker hugging close to my body, I went off and began the easier tasks. I decided to start with laundry and remember the CD I could listen while doing all this.

Finishing up the laundry, I went over to my stack and searched for Carved in Stone. I found it exactly where I had left it, on the left side of the mountain of plastic. I grabbed on to it and opened it up. Something pretty dumb to do was to check for the CD to make sure it was there in the first place, as if I could break out of its case and zip in to the to another location pretty farfetched but with all the strange crap happing around the house lately, one couldn't be too sure. I skittered over to the stereo, the anticipation practically fuming off me, and smashed the "On" button with my thumb. Come on, come on, come on. I noticed that things you want to happen, happen slower of your happy or antsy. I the tray rolled out on its track and it barely was out of the player case before I had shoved the track into it and pressed "Close". Since a CD usually plays by itself at this point I went off to the hallway closet to look for some trash bags. I came back out into the living room only to be greeted with silence. I was odd so I went over to the stereo stand and look at the player to make sure it was running. It was. All it said on the tiny display was "Track 3   1:13" and still playing, omit any sound at all. "Why start on track 3 hm? Buddy!?" I smiled, still too excited to get too angry right now and flipped through the tracks to see if they all were like this. 4 nothing. 5 nothing. 6 nothing. 7 nothing. It reset back to one now. On 1 the speakers made small hiss before beginning the song. I gave a smile and went off to my chores. The song was Rust on the Hammer. It started out with a drum set intro, pretty standard to 80's rock. Then it went into a guitar rift and a singer came on in a booming voice. I think the jist of the song is him talking about he's the best singer and rocker out there and to watch out for him. He's too cool and too proud to be stopped now. It felt so rhythmic. It soothed me but at the same time, filled me with a sort of energy.

The song continued to play while I did the dishes and vacuumed. I picked up the trash bags close to the stereo and went into the kitchen. I feel so alive. This music just hits me in my core. I started to empty out the fridge when something occurred to me. The same song was still playing. Whether or not it had repeated or was on loop I couldn't tell. I stopped what I was doing for a moment. Something took control of me. I returned to my task of cleaning out the rotten food. I couldn't stop. I just kept going and going and before I knew it I started to scrub the damn fridge out! I had no control over my actions but still it felt natural. I finished with the rest of the gunk and what not and tied the trash bags closed. I went out to throw the bags in the can outside my apartment but I could still hear that song clear as the sky. When I returned the music started to die down. I sat down just as the song ended. I tried to look to see if the song was really half an hour long or it was on loop or something but I didn't show track one. It showed track to but track 2 didn't make any sound either. I regained control of myself and tried to flip back to one. I when I had got to it, it wouldn't play. It just showed "track 1   0:00" nothing I did made it play. It didn't even make any sound at all. I was bathed in that same awkward silence. Finally getting frustrated, I turned it off and sat down on the couch. That song sounded pretty good but still. What was it about it that made it go on and on like that? Clearly I heard it, I know I did, but was it really that long? Still, it was so soothing and calming. I feel proud of the work if done today, not that I did too much. Wait, no. Not just today. Every day. I've done great these past few months. Normal people would crack under circumstances like mine. Not me! You know what? I deserve a reward. I think I'll head out and go for a nice drive in the country. That I think I need.

I shot up and went to go get ready for the second time today. I tossed on some clothes that were dirty and old tattered shoes. I didn't even think about using the same clothes I had worn in the morning or the newer shoes sitting right next to the old ones but, you know, who gives a shit. I grabbed my keys and headed out the door. I dashed to my car and jumped in the driver seat. I feel good. I'm not sure what it is but I feel really good. Confident. I revved the engine and didn't even give it time to warm up. I backed out and drove probably faster than I should have out of the complex and onto the streets. I took the first left I could and just went straight. At the pace I was going, I got into the country side pretty quick. Something started to come into focus. I sound. I could hear it faintly, then more clear.

Rust on the Hammer began to play in my head. Man that's a good song. It sounded so smooth. Made me feel invincible. I know I'm not but with this mindset, I could do anything! The buildings and telephone poles began to blur and the road seemed to stretch on into the horizon. I could feel nothing but full confidence and pride in what I do, what I've done, and who I am. I looked around to see the world curve around me. I looked at the speedometer. 140 mph. Could my car even go that fast? Could a little Toyota shit 2000 go 140 let alone 100? The numbers on the meter seemed to blur even more to me as I leaned back and sunk into the seat. I could see a rusted farm truck roll slowly up unto and intersection ahead. He'll stop. He didn't though. He continued to turn onto the road I was flying down. I had to turn. This sadistic old man wouldn't do it. Feeling no control over myself yet full of reassurance that I'd be fine, I turned slowly into the field next to me. The thing about going fast is, the faster you go, the harder to turn. The faster you go, the slightest nudge of the wheel turns you a lot more than you think. The faster you go, the road is eaten up fast. When I felt myself tap the wheel to the right, my car flew off the road and over a ditch into a field. Being in September, no crops were there but still, the slightest bump on the tires sent me bouncing like a rabbit on crack. The old man halted to a stop, his breaks squealing. He turned to look at me, a tinge of bewilderment twinkling in his eyes. I only caught a quick look at him then he disappeared from my eyesight. I turned back to look ahead of me. A concrete field marker was coming up on me as I had swerved to look at the old man and was now headed for the intersection.

The concrete markers usually protected the field and told others whose property was whose. And man are those things solid. Only four or five feet of it stick above ground but they extend about ten or fifteen feet below the surface. My foot slammed into the brake and my tires began to dig themselves in to the half frozen tilled earth. That post was getting big fast. I closed my eyes and waited for the impact. The slowed and jerked to a halt. I didn't want to look at where I was. I peeked out and saw that I was no more than a couple inches from colliding with it. My shaking hands fell from the steering wheel. The song faded in my head. What did I just do? Where was I? I slumped back in my seat and rested my head on the window. Out of my proverbial vision, I could spot a rusty old truck coming up on me from the left. The battered truck came to a stop right next to me but on the road. The old man rolled his window down and leaned over to the passenger side window.

"Good heavens man, are you alright?" His voice sounded dusty and worn. I roll down the window and glide my head to the outside of the window.

"Yea, yea, I'm fine. I think I feel asleep at the wheel. I'm ok though." He got out of his vehicle and made his way over to me.

"Would you like a tow or a ride back into town?" He asked. Trying to but as calm as possible despite my still shaking body, I replied, "No thank you. I don't think my car was damaged at all, and surely after that, I'm sure I'll stay awake."

He paused for a second, as if mulling over possible options to help this man but ultimately decided against them all. "Ok, just get home save now ya' hear?"

"Yea. Will do." He turned and began to walk back to his truck. I wanted to stop and thank this man but getting out of the car wasn't an option. I couldn't stand straight let alone form a good response. Still, I hollered over to him.

"Hey sir!" He cast a glance back then turned to face the car. "Thanks for stopping and making sure I was alright."

A small smirk crossed his face. "No problem."

"What's your name? I'm Andrew Brookstone." He came over to the side of the car and extended his hand inside the window. I met him with a firm hand myself.

"Elijah Wilkes." He said with a smile and turned away to walk back to his truck.

The whole handshake thing ended quickly since my grip loosened, blankly. What was his name again? Elijah Wilkes? Wasn't that the old man from my dream in the church? Come to think of it, he looks the same as the guy. I guess I hadn't taken any notice to him since he wasn't in his pastor get-up. Instead, he dawned a pair of overalls, Dusty blue jeans, and dark work shoes. Was it all a coincidence? Hardly. When I got into his vehicle, he turned on the radio. The song playing was so familiar. It was only after he sped off and the waves from the song came drifting through the open back window. A soothing rock song.

About half an hour later, I returned home. I took so long since I was traveling a lot slower than the speed limit because I didn't want to attract the attention of anyone who saw me earlier. I went pretty far away in the ten minutes I took to get out to nowheresville. When I went inside all was silent. Nothing out the ordinary here. Still. I wanted nothing more than this day to be over. The whole situation finally sinking in. I floated to my room and didn't even take my clothes off. I let my body collapse in the mess of blankets and sheets. Slowly, sleep filled my head and before I knew it, I was gone. Man, this felt so relaxing. The stresses of earlier melting away.

I woke early in the morning to the same beam of light that would usually wake me up in the morning and with Lilly running in with a big smile. Only today, there was no Lilly. This kind of bummed me out when I remembered that it was Janice's weekend, but at least I'd be able to go get her at around eight or so. I rolled out of bed and made my way to the kitchen still with sleep in my eyes. I went to go make some bacon and eggs. That, to me, was the best kind morning I could think of. Opening the fridge door I was greeted with a white sheet of light. I waited till my eyes adjusted and when they finally did, I cursed to myself for falling asleep and forgetting all about it. The fridge was completely empty. I had completely spaced going to the store and getting more groceries. Maybe I didn't want to. After the whole ordeal yesterday I didn't think a second longer on getting back in the car for another high speed joy ride. I'd have to go out and do it today then. So I finished waking up and got ready. Might as well knock that out before I start anything else. I grabbed my coat and keys, and right before I made it out the door, something stopped me right in my tracks. Another urge. I couldn't quite place it. I shut the door and look behind me.

Sitting on the stack of CD's was my mp3, Carved in Stone, and, who would have guessed it, tiny Jesus. Just staring at me. Begging for me to do its will. I secumed. I went over to the stack and plucked the mp3 from the top of the stack and then went for J man. I lifted him to my face and dared him to tell me his plot. If I couldn't avoid him, let him join me. I slid him in my right front jacket pocket and headed out the door. Something seemed off to me about bringing him along for the ride, like some weird taboo shit or something but oh well. He couldn't do much harm. Unless he came to life like in my dream, then I'd have nothing to worry about. Maybe he wanted to protect me even though he's a psychotic midget; he was warm and soothing to my core. I locked my door and headed for my car. I slid the keys in and the ignition didn't take long to resurrect my vehicle. From there I pulled out onto Main Street and down the road I went.

I had completely forgotten how far away the store was in this town and I might as well listen to some REGULAR music to get me through all of it before I lost my mind. I stopped at a red light with a single car ahead of me. The light had just changed to red so I think I have some time. I reached for the mp3 in my left jacket pocket and jammed the buds in my ears. I went to shuffle and put it back in my pocket. The light changed and I was off. Let's go music. You can start playing now. But all that played through the miniature speakers was a hiss. Pulling the mp3 from my pocket and glancing quickly between the road and the screen, it said my library only had seven songs. What the hell? Where my other 780 songs?! Fuck life man... The song that was currently playing was Rust on the hammer. "No." I said defiantly and shuffled through the next few songs. All the song names were not the names I had read on the case. They all said, "???". Went I returned to the main screen, having shuffled through all the songs with no luck, I clicked shuffle once more. Now instead of track 1, Rust on the Hammer, it read track 2, Take Me Away. The track was paused which I quickly remedied with the play button. Hopping it would play on its own, I shifted my gaze back to the road. Then the intro kicked in, which I was thankful for.

It began with a flute and clarinet opening. Classical? Hm, interesting. Still, I made me feel welcome, so to speak. Then, a powerful brass section faded in then out. Nice crescendo decrescendo. I know my music. Some violins and fiddles came into effect now, with a fancy piano accompaniment and from there on out seemed to take the feel of some Victorian mansion. "Oooo." Fancy fancy. Well done sire's Messiah of Silver. You must know to right audience." I say out loud to myself. I finally pulled in to the Shop N' Mart...um...mart and came to a rest in the closest spot I could find to the store. I got out of my car making sure I had everything; wallet, keys, jacket, Jesus, mp3, and the rest of me. The music still played. It seemed to be around the same length as Rust on the Hammer. I didn't mind. Because of the fancy dancy music playing in my ears, I practically strolled up into the store, feeling smart and full of myself. I made my way around the mart faster than I remember and swiped my card in the thing-a-ma-jig and left with my bundle of items.

I got to my car and popped the trunk open with the button on my keychain. At this point, the music had faded then stopped. I came back from my high on life feeling to reality. What...? What's all this crap doing in my cart? I take in sight of the massive mound of different foods and other miscellaneous shit pilling up more and more the more I stare it. I had foods and different boxes of things I could hardly pronounce let alone eat. I spot my recipe at the frayed edges of my jean pockets and rip it from its hold. 604.65$!? This is outrageous! I didn't want all this! This is enough food to feed an entire football team for a month! I momentarily thought of coming back through those sliding doors, slamming the recipe down on the counter in front of the cashier and making them feel terrible about themselves but what good would that do? Leave me in the dark with a normalized bank account and a stained conscience? Nah, I'll be fine.

It took me fifteen minutes to Tetris all the different food items properly in the trunk, backset, and passenger seat, doing my best to not crush the breads or leave the soaps to the meats and what not. When I got in my car I sighed and a realization came to me. This shit's heavy. I felt I foot shorter in my already small car. This was going to suck trying to haul all of this home. My mpg will surely hate me when this was all over. Getting out of the parking lot and onto the road, I figured out I was right. I needed gas. So I pulled in the nearest Quicky's and filled my tank to the brim. Again, more than I needed or had the money for after splurging on this pluffer of food over flowing my car but still. I didn't care. I got home and went to unlock the door. The silence still making itself present in the home. It took longer to get all the crap inside than it took to put it in the car. It was all in and I put it all away. I slumped into the couch and rested my eyes, trying relax after that straining task. Once again, a noise faded into my head. Take Me Away was dancing its way into my head.

My body began to come over the control of something I clearly didn't like. I stood and went straight for the kitchen. I grabbed some of the things I had just bought, bags of chips, drinks, chicken, and random other foods I didn't mean to buy. I threw them on the couch and sat on a bag of chips. I didn't care. I began to gorge myself in all the fantastic things I got. My face was stuffed in seconds and still shoveling in more. Soon my stomach hurt. It told myself to stop and slow down but I ignored. My teeth rattled and my gums were stressed an hour later when I called it quits. The song, once again, faded away. Oh crap...Ow....ow...Ow.OW...OWOWOWWOWOOW! My stomach kills! I let out a groan of pain and fell forward onto the floor. My stomach hated me. "Why are you being so irrational and eating all this food?!" It screamed at me. I don't know tummy, I don't know. It apparently wasn't happy with my answer and fought back. I empty all that I had eaten onto the floor below me. Two, three times. Now my guts hurt. I different pain. It came from my abdomen. I ran to the bathroom and emptied more. That was the worst shit I had ever taken. I fell to the floor outside the bathroom afterwards and felt exhausted. My vision back to fade.

I awoke a few hours later with the noxious smell of something. Duh. My stomach leavings still fermenting on the carpet. I sat up and clenched my nose with my hand. Awful. I stoop wearily and went to go some cleaning things. My trusty tools by my side, Windex, Bounty Paper Towels, and Frebreeze by my side, I began the fight against the awful mess I had made. I never want to have to do that again. I threw the used items away and sat on the couch. Awww man... The food is still here and some of it is starting to rot. Nasty. I threw that away and put other things in the cabinets and went to my room. I lie down on my bed and close my eyes. I felt like shit man. I opened my eyes and stared at the ceiling. A few moments later I felt an ever increasing weight in my front right jacket pocket.

I look down to see a hint of silver poking out of my pocket. I pull the tiny Jesus out and hold him above my head to look at him for a sec. What is all that on him? Clearly the silver little man had been dipped in mud while I wasn't looking. I got up and flicked the light switch on. Rust. Rust was now covering his lower part of his body. The damaged reached up past his robe shrouded knees and was extensive. The rust under his chin had stayed the same but the new damage was shocking to say the least. I know I hadn't feel in any puddles of water lately and I also know that I didn't vomit on myself to make this happen. Were the rust resided was starting to crater in, as if more than just a few grams of silver had worn away, and was now eating deep into the iron underneath. What. The. Hell. MAN?!?! I got angry at this for some reason. I think it was an awful idea to bring the man with me on my daily chores. I think HE made me do what I did. I clenched my fist around him and stormed outside. I threw him at the fence out on the back porch and hit landed with a solid thud in the earth. "Fuck you." I proclaimed and went inside. I shut and locked the door behind me.

I came to a rest on the kitchen counter, still rittled with varying sizes of food items that didn't fit anywhere else in the cabinets, cupboard, or fridge. I rested my elbows on the counter and my head, softly in my hands. I am so stressed out right now. It's destroying me. I'm just so done. My calm demeanor slowly but surely fading in a grim and forbidding state. I need to talk to someone. Anyone. I reached for my phone and scrolled through my contacts. Only one stuck out of all the different names and numbers, Jessica. She would understand. Even if I had to pay to talk to her. She wasn't paid to talk to her clients about their personal lives to deeply, just deep enough to get the facts. I'm pretty sure she wouldn't mind though. Me and her are forming a sort of friendship, if I can say. I clicked call and let the phone ring. Once, twice, three times, a forth, "Hello you've-" "Jessica?" I hurriedly said cutting the recording off. "-reached the office of Jessica S. Lacy. I'm not in at the moment, but if you would leave your name, phone number, and time of calling, I'll get back to you as soon as I can. Thanks!" Then it cut back to the "if you'd like to leave a message" crap. I pressed end and slid the phone, depressed, back in my pocket. Even Jessica couldn't, wouldn't, talk to me. I returned to my original pose. The depression emanating from me. I gloomily looked up at the oven clock. 6:53 it read. Oh crap! I have to get ready to go get Lilly! I hastily grabbed my jacket and shoes and sprinted for my car. Did I lock it? Who cares. I gota' go go go! I hopped in the car and raced off to the usual rendezvous.

I arrived a little after eight with a white SUV waiting for me, like a bully ready to beat up some kid right after school. I pulled in beside her and cast a look over into the other window. Though it was tinted and dark out, I could still make out the faces of Janice and Lilly in the car, the blue glow from the stereo lighting up their features. Lilly leaned in and gave what I made out to be a kiss on the cheek to her mother and the door opened. Lilly slammed the door shut and made her way over to my passenger side door. she turned and gave one last wave before hopping inside my car and throwing her things in the back seat.

"Hellooooo there dad." She turned and gave a full-hearted smile. I smiled back and gave her a hug.

"How are you doing?" I asked as the white monster rolled away and me following behind but going in the other direction.

"Oh, pretty good, pretty good. And you?" She might have meant it but still, she seemed zoned out and was now staring out the window at the passing landscape. I thought about what she said for a minute or two. Should I tell her or should I just leave it be... I didn't want to worry her but I also wanted to tell someone to get this off my chest. I mulled over this for a minute and finally turned to her. She seemed to notice the length it took me to respond and was already facing me, waiting for an answer.

"I'm doing alright myself. Pretty quiet around the house while you were gone but I was able to manage." I smirked and turned back to the road. "You know how all that food went bad?"

"Yea?" More of a question than a response.

"Well I cleaned all that crap out of there and bought some more food to fill it back up." The smirk still dancing on my lips since it was, when I think about it, pretty funny, the whole situation. The food being rotten, thrown out, just to be replaced by a monstrous amount of food, then being sort of eaten as soon as it was bought.

"What if it goes bad again? Do you know what caused it?" She said without hesitation.

Her comment hit me with such a blow that the air in my lungs seemed to get caught in my throat. The thought never crossed my mind. What had caused it all to happen? I'm not sure. Was it that the fridge went bad? I think a better explanation is that damned Jesus. I think it is a curse. I just happened to be the poor bastard who it fell into the hands of. Was that it? Did I really buy a cursed Jesus? Seemed to me sort of ironic if you think about it. And what's with that music? Did that have something to do with it? It's as if when I play a song, something bizarre and outrageous happens, between the confidence in my driving abilities or the buying and consumption of the stockpile of food. Maybe I shouldn't listen to my mp3 anymore. It'd be rough, but maybe by next paycheck I could get another. Lilly was again looking to me for an answer.

"Hm. Not sure. Guess I'll have to clean it out again and buy more food." She pondered the response well before returning to her window view.

The rest of the ride was pretty silent. I was silent because of my unsure mind and mounting stress, Lilly because of physical exhaustion. I'm not sure why, be she seemed pretty tired when she came back from Janice's. I could only stretch my mind so far as to think that Janice made her work to the bone. So we rode and arrived in silence and made our way up to the apartment. I unlocked it and made our way inside. The numbing silence was broken by our shuffling feet and rustling of clothes and bags. She scampered off to her room and I took my place at the far end of the couch. I flicked the TV on and starting dulling my mind with dumb shows. Lilly went off to take a shower and I thought it was about the time to start dinner. She didn't like to eat at her mother's since Janice didn't really buy the foods that Lilly liked. I didn't give into all of her cravings but I did give her some leeway. I got up and started to make some beef stew for me and some stroganoff for her. I set the table and waited patiently in the living room, leaving the food unattended.

She was still in the shower. What the deuce? How long does it take for a teenage girl to take a shower? I was starting to get hungry. I went in and grabbed a full bag of chips. I began to munch on them and the shower shut off. Just in time too. The door stayed firmed shut. A few noises made their way out of the bathroom then the light went off inside there. What is she doing in there? I got up and went over to the door and knocked. "Lilly? What are you doing in there?" No answer. I opened the door, unnerved to find it unlocked and was met with darkness. I flicked the light on and no one was inside. The curtain was splayed and I could see no one was there. "Lilly?" I called out.

"What do you want dad?" I heard from her room. I turned the light off and speed walked to her door.

"Lilly you in there?" I said.

"Duh." She retorted sarcastically.

"What are you doing in there?" My mind more than a little confused.

"Getting dressed. Duh. Gimme' a minute and I'll be out."
Uh? She was in there? Who was in the bathroom then? I
grabbed my bag of chips and went to the kitchen, my mind still
a haze. Too much weird shit is going on lately. I need to find
out what. Even if I can just talk to someone about this. I need
to get this burden off my shoulders. Lilly came out a few
minutes later dressed in sweatpants and a tank top. We sat
and ate and by ten, both of us where completely wiped out.
She went to bed and I soon followed, retreating to mine,
making sure to shut down the TV and lights as well as locked
the doors. I lay down and pulled the sheets over my body and
tried to rest. Tomorrow I had work. Another mind numbing
week ahead of me, and with no music at that! My eyes shut
and sleep soon took a hold of me. I dreamed of music that
night. Songs. Two in particular. Rust on the Hammer and Take
Me Away.

Chapter 6: Horrid Revelations

5:30 rolls around and it's time for me to get up. I didn't get a wink of sleep last night. Those damn songs played for hours in my head. I couldn't get them to stop. The dream itself told me of hard times to come and that this was just the beginning. I was just a piece of the puzzle. Something larger was afoot. For hours, days even, my mind became some sort of fucked up prophet. All of it is unnerving however. Even though I know it's just a dream, it still scared the shit out of me. I remember being told that no matter what I did, I could not escape my fate. The "Rust" is eating away at my soul and would soon fully consume me. I'm taking no risks. I don't want my mind to be true. For once, I want it to mislead me.

Lilly came in as usual with a cup of coffee in one hand and shoved me a few times with the other to try to shake me from my sleep. A smile was on her face, which always made me light up on the morning.

"Morning! Get a move on mister!" She beamed at me.

"Fine, fine." I mumbled, took the coffee and rolled out of bed.

A painful feeling was creeping it's way into my thoughts. I felt somehow off. I still got up and got ready for the day. Emerging from my room, I took a seat at the kitchen table to enjoy a warm breakfast that Lilly had prepared. Time passed and Lilly was out the door to school. I finish up cleaning and getting ready and before I know it, I myself was out the door. I open my car and sit in the driver's seat and fish around my pocket for my keys. I wait for the car to warm up. Hurry up... Come on... I want to be done with this day already. I close my eyes trying to get a wink more of sleep. The heat was on and only usually take off when it gets warm enough. I felt the temperature reaching that point so I open my eyes.

My mp3 is sitting near the meters and J man is sitting on the dash. What the hell? I grabbed the tiny man in a fist of hate and glared down at him. "What do you think you're doing here huh buddy?" I say, defying him. He's resting in my fist with a few chunks of rust coming off. I roll the window down and chuck him out into the cold. He hit the pavement with a crack, sending more rusted chunks flying around him. "Crazy sadistic fuck!" I thought I had left him in the backyard. Crazy thing is following me. Maybe when I get home, I'll saw him up and melt him down. He'd sure make a good paperweight. My hand reaches for the stick shift and click it into reverse. I hurriedly back out, throw it into drive, and speed off. I don't think going that fast was that necessary but I don't know why I wouldn't at the same time.

The ride began quiet and calm. More quiet than normal since the lack of music was ever so present. I was almost settled in for the long haul when something began to bump. A deep bass. Vibrating from a few feet in front of me. It was coming from the mp3. The sound was abnormally loud for the tiny waves coming from the buds but still it was enough to rock the mp3. It began to get in rhythm with the bass and began to move off the dash. It fell and started to dance around the floor with that same bass playing. I couldn't look away from the road to stop it from moving, so I let it bounce around. It stopped for a minute. It resumed after a man with a deep bombing voice said a few lines. The man in the recording sounded young. He wasn't black, despite being a rap sound, he was white. I'm pretty sure I can tell just by the inflections in his voice. The bass coupled with the rapping man went on for a bit before stopping and saying what I'd assume was the main verse of the whole song:

"Find me in the shady mist,

stuck on the rotten bark.

You'll find the silver in my wrists,

Come alone, half past dark."

After those lines the bass ensued and was returned to the original lines and groove. What did he mean by stuck on rotten bark? And how about the next line, you'll find the silver in my wrists? That sounds familiar. Duh. That was the song name. I remember reading it on the case. I came to a stop in my parking spot at work and turned the key off, choking the life from my car. As the car finally coughed its last few breaths, the mp3 died down slowly, too. The music faded out leaving only the heavy bass in its wake. After one last bump, the bass shut off and was replaced by a loud hiss. Now I had a chance to grab the mp3. The screen said that song on queue was Track 4. The hiss was the standby sound of the speakers being turned up so high. A sudden pop made me drop the music player, the noise taking me by surprise. That was the sound of the speakers cutting out and being blown out. Great... Now there REALLY was no music to listen to.

I left the dumb thing in the car and hauled my way to the main plaza of my dead end job. What do you know? Chuck was coming out of his office with the same musky clothes he's being wearing for weeks now with an armful of paperwork. He was dropping a few of them and stumbling a bit. I could faintly hear the echo of a mumble in the plaza. He looked to the side of his path and spotted me coming in the doorway. As soon as he saw me, he immediately seemed to grin. He threw the papers down on a nearby table and starting fishing through the mountainous stack. I tried to hurry past without him stopping me but unfortunately, he ran and blocked my path. He held out a single piece of paper. A work order.

"Oh, Andrew! Glad I caught you. You need to take this call." Ew... His greasy sticky fingers are seeping onto the paper.

"I can't Mr. Warburton, I've got my own calls to attend to at my desk on top of the papers I need to input into the computer."

"No time, this one has been sitting in here for hours. Money is money. Go do it before she changes her mind."

"Get someone else to do it, I'm busy." I try and amble out of the way of the sticky wall but he kept me from passing.

"Do it anyway." He stopped me with a firm hand. "No one else will be back in time and you're not busy RIGHT now. Get going before I kick your ass to the curb." He didn't seem smug today, he seemed infuriated. I think I was right in my assumption of someone coming out here and threatening him with his job over his head.

"Fine." I snatched it out of his hand and he collected all of his papers and was on his way.

I turned the paper over and read the description. It was a woman in her 80's with a decently sized house for being a widow. She wanted to put in a new kitchen with a rework of all the pipes and gas lines for the stove. Come to think of it, this was the same woman who I went to look around her bathroom. This girl was loaded! I had no idea where she got all of it but sure as hell spent it well. Something inside me jumped at the opportunity. I could have went to find someone to pass it off to but something told me I should go, you know... look around... I threw my things down on my desk and donned my work polo. I was out the door and in the car in mere minutes. I sped off in the direction of the home. I can't wait to get there! The silence of the car was numbing. After I pulled into the driveway and shut off the key, I was just about to step out but something stopped me. A faint bass in my head. Bump. Bump. Bump. Silence. It hadn't really deterred me but still slowed me up to the front door. I rang the doorbell and a small, quiet, speak came from inside what I could tell the living room.

"Coming. One moment." The voice sounded dry and withered. The same old woman opened the door and smiled up at me. I knew she trusted me which somehow made me grin.

"Oh! It's you! Oh, please come on in. Would you like a cup of tea before you get to work?" She beamed at me and slowly made her way to the kitchen.

"Sure! Why not!" I beat her to the kitchen, sort of cutting her off. She didn't seemed to notice, but I did. It was rude but I didn't care. She started the tea and I took a seat at the table.

"Make yourself at home now."

"Oh of course!" She put a cup of tea on the table in front of me. I gulped it down and asked for another cup. She quickly filled it again and I finished that cup off too.

"My my, thirsty today? Oh well. Would you like to begin looking around?" She said as she started out of the kitchen. She didn't even want to watch me. Sweet!

I stood and left the chair cooked to the side. I pulled my notepad out and began inspecting the walls and pipes underneath the sink. Silver in my Wrists faded into my minds ear. I stopped what I was doing for a minute, sort of taken aback by the catchy bass line and the lyrics. My foot started tapping and my head started bobbing with the beat. I stood up, leaving my notepad on the ground and started to look around the house. This wasn't my curiosity, it was the songs. I made my way to the bedroom and started to investigate. This chick was loaded, she has to have some money chilling out somewhere. There on the nightstand, I spotted what looked to be the stereotypical old granny purse. I snatched it from its resting place and started fumbling around inside looking for anything that either I could sell or maybe just pocket. My fingers rested on a faded money clip and I ripped it from the purse. Without thinking, I tossed it in my pocket and left the purse on the bed. What else, what else. There was a jewelry box close to a mirror and I flipped it open. Gems. Shiny rocks stuck to different colored and curved rings and necklaces. Fake or not, I liked them. I tucked them snuggly in my back pocket and didn't even care to shut the lid of the box.

"She's cleaned out." I said to myself. "This will cover the cost of me wasting my time here. Whatever, she gets her clearance and what not." I went around the house and found her deeply interested in a book in the living room. Good thing the hallway to her bedroom wasn't in line of sight of the living room. As I came in, she noticed me and said.

"What's the plan Stan?" A smile still dancing on her lips. Poor ignorant bitch.

"Oh, you're clear to do the renovations. I'll leave a copy of the clearance sheet with you and I'll take the other back with me." I handed her a half-ass filled out sheet. She didn't know that it was half filled out but she was just the innocent old lady needing some help. She didn't know any better.

"Oh great! Well I don't suppose you're headed back now hm?"

"Yup, I got a lot of other places to get to in the wee hours of the day. Yea, I got to get going. I'll give you a call in a few days to let you know what's going on.

"Alrighty then. You take care now. Bye!" And with that last comment of hers I was out the door and on the path back to the car. The heavy bass was still bumping in my head with a vengeance.

I finally reached my Toyota and sat in the driver's seat. With a bass in my head and a wheel in my hands, I made my way back to my parking spot at work. The song in my head faded and was replaced by the eerie silence. What just happened? I got out of my car and went in. I arrived at my desk and slumped in my chair. I felt something poking out of my pocket. Scratch that, pockets. I reached in my front pocket to find a clip of cash. Scared, I went for my back pocket. Pointed shiny rocks and rings filled my hand. Did I steal these? What did I do?! I threw the various rock at the wall and hit like rain on a metal roof. The clip fell from my hand and plummeted to the floor. I backed out of my cubical and stood a few feet from the station. I peered around. No one else was in the area near my cubical. I quickly grabbed the merchandise and ran out of the building.

I arrived at my car once again. I tossed the goods to the seat next to me and roared the engine to life. I was just about to turn the stick to drive but something caught my eye. My hands. They were shaking, and bad. I closed my eyes and did the best I could to calm down. I couldn't go driving around with an unsteady hand now could I? A few minutes passed and I felt I had regained control of myself. I pulled from the parking spot and sped off in the direction of the old lady's house. Not ten minutes had passed till I had came to a weary stop at the mailbox. My hand reached to the seat next to me and grabbed a handful of her goods. I chucked them in to the box and slammed it shut. The least I could do was to give this crap back. Just because I wasn't thinking when I stole it, didn't mean I had to stay a thief.

The old woman peeked through her curtains at her front window which scared me pretty bad, like seeing a ghost. I immediately pushed the pedal to the floor and drove away, tires screeching. A few blocks away, I saw her get to the mailbox and look inside in my rear view mirror. She pulled some of the things out and physically remembered them then turned to stare at the car peeling away from the scene of the crime. Her face gave it away. She was astounded, relived, and furious. I couldn't stand her gaze a moment longer. I turned from the mirror back to the road. Guilt filled my mind to the brim with pain. I didn't mean to do it. I wasn't all "there". Surely she couldn't blame me for mental instability. It wasn't me...It wasn't...It...it was...THAT DAMN SONG!

It did this to me! Come to think of it, all of the things I've done recently have made me do things out of my will! That explains the robbery, the stockpile and consumption of food and the near head on collision with a concrete barrier! Well...! Actually...No...It didn't explain anything. The most I could piece together was that whenever I listen to one of those songs, something completely wild and unpredictable happens.

I might be able to stop this this time around. If I completely avoid any type of music, I should be in the grass green clear! The whole idea made sense in my mind but who knows, I'm off my rocker at the moment. I couldn't think straight about anything. I could just be experiencing a mid-life crisis. Could I? Doubtful. I'm like, 33. No record, that I can think of, of mental instability in my family tree. No clue. For starters though, the mp3 and CD have GOT TO GO.

I came to a abrupt halt at my parking spot at home. It was early, but I couldn't go back to work. That old lady will mostly likely be hunting around for me. She seemed quiet and nice enough but also seemed like one of those people that if you provoke that they come at you with knives in hand. I opened the door to my home. Quiet, still, petrified air hung gloomily in the room. All the rooms. Although, somehow this was normal as well as comforting. It matched me, this stillness. I flopped onto the couch and flipped the TV on. Hours of mind numbing static and pixels ought to cool my heels. Some crafting show was on, not surprising in the least. It was the middle of the day and nothing was ever on this time of day. The pixels began to fade together and my eyelids became tremendously heavy. They fell onto my eye socket and sleep took my by the hand. Sometime later, I was rudely awoken by a slam of a door and a high pitched squeal.

"Aaaafffttterrrrnoooonnn dad." Lilly said and gave me a hug on the couch. Me, still being semi-asleep didn't really fully comprehend the hug but it did vaguely register.

"Afternoon doll. How was school?"

"Oh, alright. Boring but it's whatever. Nothing new." Well, still a crappy answer but no parent really argued of the half-assed story telling of the day.

I rubbed the last bit of sleep from my eyes. "Why don't you get yourself something to eat. I'm wiped so I might just go back in my room and hibernate in there.

"Mk. Whatever ya' silly." She bounded off to her room for a second or two and remerged only to go straight for the kitchen. I picked my sorry self up and Frankenstein walked to my room. The door shut softly behind me, my hand not letting it hit to hard. I made a bee line for my bed. "Ah, sleep. I return to you. Make me a samich'" I was weird like that. I closed my eyes and feel hoping the bed would cushion my fall and I'd fall right back to sleep. Nope. Not this time pally.

I was met with an intense pain starting in my nose and reverberating throughout my entire body. I coiled out on my side, my hands making a race to my face seeing which one would make it there first to comfort me. It hurt immensely. After throwing a few hate words blindly into the air, I sat up on the bed, my hands still cradling my poor, poor nose. Lilly came crashing through the door and gave a rather loud shriek.

"Oh my god dad! Are you alright? What's wro...*Shriek* Oh shit dad, your nose!" She came over to me and tried to get a better look but I firmly held her at bay with a rough hand pushing the air in front of her at her. She stopped and got down to see if she could see my nose. All she saw was a dark liquid coming from the crevices between my fingers. She left the room and returned moments later with an armful of paper towels, rags and disinfectants. Man this really hurt alot. She shoved alot of it at me and I took the nearest towel and held it to my face.

"Ow. This hurts a lot, Lilly. I can harbly breeb." My voice sounded like Squidward's or something with this rag clogging up my nose. I stood and went into the bathroom to get a better look at my wound. I flicked the light on and even I was a little shocked. Well, for starters, the rag on my face, once white as snow, now was red as rose. It was covered in the center with blood and different splotches were dotting the outside of it. My hands were bloody as well as my shirt. If you saw me, you wouldn't be able to tell if I had just came from ripping someone's organs out and happily enjoying them without having the courtesy of cleaning up after myself. I removed the rag from my face slowly, as to not throw blood around the bathroom and give it a dashing new wall color. Almost right I wanted to put my hands back, out of pure fright of the damage that has been done. My nostril had been smashed to the side with blood simply gushing from my nose, no shocker there. On my face however was a mark, not like a fancy tattoo or a creative and fortuitous injury. Right between my eyes and above my nose was a heart, or maybe a bag, I'm not entirely sure, with sunshine markings shooting from it. The symbol was small and innocuous but still was no normal injury. I too was bleeding, not bad though, just cut open.

I had to hurry up and fix this before the nose began to heal in such a way. I took another wash cloth and rinsed it with some water. I began to clean the blood from my face and hands. The shirt I couldn't care less about. I've got plenty of these polo's. With the majority of the blood gone, I grabbed my nose, closed my eyes, and braced myself before snapping it forcefully back into place. I started to bleed again but that didn't really matter that much, I had set it back. Now if it stayed there, it would heal properly. I kept cleaning up after myself, trying to stay ahead of the rushing blood and eventually, I did win the fight. The bleeding subsided and I took the rag and finished cleaning the last of the blood. Lilly came into the bathroom to check up on me.

"Y'all' right now?" She asked with concern in her eyes and worry in her words.

"Yea, yea I'm fine. I set the nose so now it should heal right." She seemed relived at the thought and site of a cleaned up dad.

"I think I found what you landed on." She inquired. Apparently, she had something behind her back.

"Yea?"

"Your tiny Jesus man." She held it a couple feet in front of her face, in a way asking for me to take it. My heart stopped and without thinking, I snatched it from her hands and threw it across the bathroom. It impaled itself in the wall with a loud *thunk* and a plume of dust. Lilly screamed out of reaction. Why did I throw it? Reaction. I'm so done with him! Hope he burns... I stood there staring at the wall; Lilly was burning holes with her eyes in me and in the wall with pure bewilderment. She snapped out of it and yelled.

"WHAT THE HELL WAS THAT FOR!?" Anger tinged a little in her voice. The noise made me cringe just a bit. I turned to her.

"I...I have no idea..."

"You just threw a Jesus statue in our wall! What made you do that!?" Yup, anger was rising and falling in her voice as she spoke.

"I...Um...Don't..."

"Don't give me that!"

"I don't know!" I responded rather loudly.

The house fell silent. Hurt and confusion lurked behind Lilly's eyes. She turned and went off to her room. She slammed the door shut. I was left alone in the bathroom, with just my fuzzy thoughts to comfort me. I took one last look in the direction of the hole. Something caught my eye. I went over to the embedded man and wiggled him free of the wall. His chest was what caught my attention. A symbol he was pointing to with his left hand. That's what I landed on. I must have hit dead center on him and that's how I got hurt. But again...WHY THE HELL WAS HE THERE IN THE FIRST PLACE!? I threw him outside in the cold and left him to rot. Well, break down and chip into dust. Come to think of it, he seemed even more rusted now. It was spreading around him, making various rings around his body. I am so done with this silver menace. I stormed out of the bathroom shutting the light off, and going to my room. In my closet, I had a gun safe. I didn't own any guns but still, these things are impossible to open or break into. I wheeled the latch to the combination and the door opened with ease. I tossed him in and shut it hard. That'll learn him.

Now I was tired. I wanted nothing more to do than go back to my bed and let this day end. Too much bad shit has happened today and I just want to forget the whole thing. I went to go lay down but I pieced together I probably couldn't, given the current situation of the bed. The bed was just covered in my blood with chunks of small things sticking from the sea. I leaned in closer to see what they were. Rust, they were tiny rust chunks. The force of the impact must have knocked a few loose pieces free. "Fine..." I sigh to myself and rip the sheets from the bed. Luckily, the blood hasn't yet reached the mattress yet so I was in pretty good shape. I tossed the covers aside and laid on the bare bed. The raw material of the mattress wasn't the greatest and sure was itchy but all in all pretty comfy. Not being able to stay awake another minute, I collapse unto the bed. as I lay, sleep already was waiting in a taxi to take me to soothing dreams.

What seemed like hours later, I awoke. I was cold, freezing actually, it was dark. Wind was hitting my face. What? Wind? What is this crap? My eyes opened as well as my senses and I felt the stabbing of splintery wood all around me. Water hit my face in waves, more misting than anything. I sat up quickly and found I was clearly not in my bed. I was on a boat. A small boat. In the middle of the sea. Nothing was around me for as far as I could see. The wind was kicking up and water hit me in the face again. I'm stranded! Oh crap someone save me! I thought to myself. I couldn't speak, the words wouldn't come out. So I just yelled with my thoughts. All the stimulants around me were mind bending to take in at once. The noise was getting increasing louder. I held my hears shut and closed my eyes trying to cut the connection of sight and sound from my senses to calm me down. I didn't help. The wind was getting louder and the ship became more and more instable. I would die in this boat before to long, or worse yet, lose my mind completely and go completely mad.

Just as I thought that I was about to lose that last strand of sanity, the noise dulled a bit. The boat began to rock slower. The water was hitting me lethargically and the wind was brushing the air from my face smoothly. I felt like I was in a time warp in space...and in an ocean. With the noise now almost completely faded in my head a new sound arose. It was slow. An acoustic guitar began to ring out above the waves, sounding fairly similar to a song playing over dozens of speakers in a mall. I slow voice of an aged man could now be heard, singing calming lyrics. I removed my hands from my ears and opened my eyes a bit wider. The atmosphere seemed to answer to the words of the man and the weather got in sync with this man's booming vocalizations. I actually sat back in the boat and rested my head on the side. I simply watched the world around me revolve. I began to catch on the lyrics and began to hum a beat out loud. I was getting calmer and calmer as time went on. I sat and observed the ocean roar and spit all around me in slow motion. I didn't care. I was feeling peaceful and tranquil, maybe even tired. I could just sleep while all this went on.

I thought that was a good idea so I laid flat on the planks. So peaceful. The sky was still dark, a few stars poked out of the clouds. The guitar slowed and the voice did to making the words ever more the clearer. I heard these lyrics:

As life does tumble;

and the clouds do rumble,

never let life make your bright mind dry.

Make life vibrant, and lift me high!

As the last words "lift me high!" were spoken, a wave came underneath me and lifted the boat up. Life picked up its regular pace and everything shot back to real time. Out of reaction, my arms shot to the sides of the boat in an attempt to brace myself. The wave lifted me higher and higher. As I reached the peak of the wave, the boat shuttered and began to turn on its side. I was essentially becoming a reverse sail to this wave. I began to fall, with the force of the wave behind me, straight down into the ocean. when I was nearing the top of the water, a rock was revealed out of the murky abyss. The wave retracted the water and made the rock more clear. In seconds I was flung towards the rock and hit face first on the charcoal colored stone.

I awoke on the floor covered in sweat and blood coming from my nose. I must have fallen off the bed and landed on the ground hard enough to get it going again. "God damn it." I thought to myself. All I'm feeling is shock. I look at the time. Three in the morning. I hate to say it, but I need to get back to sleep. Work was in a few hours. With as tired as I've been lately, I can't afford to come to work tired or worse, fall asleep on the job. Mr. Warburton has given me plenty of warnings lately and if I were to fuck up one more time, I can kiss my job goodbye.

I crawl back in bed, pull the sheets over me, and try and go back to sleep. Maybe this wouldn't affect me and I'd be fine. Come on body, sleep! For hours, it seemed, I laid there in the dark. I can't sleep. Not after that fucked up dream and the recent events. For some reason, that dream messed me up. Seems like hours...just lying there. The darkness clawing at me above the sheets. I toss and turn forever. How long have I been laying here? I glance at the clock. The numbers are blurred, I can't quite make them out. Probably due to the fact I'm almost asleep. I shrug it off and go back to enduring the tortuous night. Guess I'll have to try my hardest today to stay awake.

My eyes are cracked open at the unexpected sunlight. What time was it? I throw a look at my clock. Nine! Nine in the morning! I'm so late! I hurriedly try and get ready. My phone makes a blipping noise. This stops me. What...Oh no...I begrungly retrieve the device from my pocket and worriedly look at it. Holy crap! It's tomorrow already! I've been asleep for two days! Three new voice mails, all from yesterday. The number...That pig of a boss of mine. I put down my socks I was going to put on and take a seat at the corner of my bed. I click call for voice mail and click speaker on, just to be sure and crystal of the words I was to hear.

"First unheard message." The recorded woman said.

"Andrew? This is Mr. Warburton. Where are you? No one is in here again and the orders are piling up! Get in here right now. My fuse is already short and you don't need to make it any worse." After that it ended. Not as bad as I thought it would be, since he's usually pretty negative. Still, he can't be happy I'm not there. My mind still shaky and holding on by a mere thread, I click on the next message.

"Second unheard message." Here we go. I hold my breath and hop for the best.

"Andrew! Were the hell are you! No phone call? No "I'm sick boss, I can't come in."? Didn't even tell anyone? Who do you think you are just not coming into work. I'm so tired of your crap Andrew! You know what, YOUR DONE! Your sorry ass is gone. Good luck finding somewhere else to work you sorry fuck, cause you're sure as shit not getting a job here again!" With that the recording ended. I place my head in my hands and shed a few tears. A defeated sigh makes its way out of my lungs.

"Third unheard message." What...I raise my teary head and look at the phone as if it was a person. Staring into its face, it started to speak its words.

"Andrew, how are you? Feeling alright son? You haven't come back yet and the builders haven't either." The voice was...familiar. It sounded riddled with age. Bumps and cracks could be felt as the words passed through my ears.

"You said you'd be back in a few days and when you didn't come back, I decided to give you a call and see what is wrong." This...this man was...Father Wilkes from the church. Also, I-I think, Elijah, the old man in the rusty old truck. I didn't give him my number. What did he want? What di-

"Is it that racket of music you listen to? Can't believe you got one of those... So awful and harmful. Not good for your health you see. Makes one go mad you may have noticed. I surely feel bad you've listened to four of the seven songs. Most can't even survive that long. You must be truly suffering right now. Any matter, I think you remember me. I also believe you know how I know all this."

All the air from my lungs are gone. He crushed them with his blatant words. He knew I had a Carved in Stone CD? He knew how many songs I've heard? He knew I was suffering. That's sure as hell true. But how? I can feel it...I know it's true...Mind is unhinging slowly. He's doing it so subtly. I-It's impossible. Keep it together Andrew. It's all in your head...It's all in your head...IT'S ALL IN YOUR HEAD! I keep repeating over and over in my head. The recording seemed to pause, as if giving me this time to gather my thoughts. What a foolish attempt at this it was. The longer the silence lasted, the more my mind became unstable.

"I know all this from my helpful friend. You bought him not too long ago. He's a direct connection to your thoughts you know. The more you pray to him, the stronger that connection gets. The more you worry and think about him, the stronger he gets. Feeding off you fear and despair. Oh come now, you must know of him. His striking resemblance of that bastard above is too much to ignore."

No...not THAT. All this time. A-after all this time, it was that small silver shit.

"Ah, I see. you do know him." What? Did he hear that!?

"Yes Andrew. Don't fear me. I'm here to help." The last bit of tears dried from my face and now I'm glaring into the phone. He was real.

"What the fuck are you?" I say, shaking and fright stricken

"I'm just a man. More a prophet. I'm also a rather enthusiastic music fan. I was in a band once. Ha. That fell apart quick. You may know them."

"I-I...Um..."

"Don't think to much on it. Back to the point at hand. Andrew. I've been watching you. I'm always there, in forms that may not make sense to you. That object has a connection to you, as well as me. Both of us are bonded with the object as the siphon and connector. I can feel it. That's the way it's made. Your thoughts, I can read them. I see what you see. I feel what you feel. Your fear, it's a grand thing. Never have I felt so much courage clashing with terror in one's head. It's filling. Though you seem to be spent. Your mental state is declining fast and your body is worn. It's a shame you've been marked this early."

"Marked?" I respond. Marked for what? What was going on here?

"Yes, marked. I believe you know of the mark. It happened not to long ago actually. You must know. I felt it too." I briefly recall the bloodied mark between my eyes.

"Yes, that mark. It means that you no longer have any will to continue. Your life is over. You have nothing to live for anymore."

"But Lilly! I have her! You have no idea what I stand for! Here it is! I live for her! I put up all crap to see her happy!"

"Ah but you'd throw your life away at the same time. You don't deserve to continue on. You must be ended. You will is broken, your mind is unhinged, and your emotions are sporadic. At this rate, she'd be taken away within days! I will save you however."

"Fuck you! You have now power over me!" I throw the phone down and run towards my bedroom door. My hands fumble with the knob but nothing happens. "Come on! Open!"

"It's no use Andrew. I control your actions now. Nothing can save you from my wrath. If you want to take your fury out on something before you part from this world with it all, attempt to break our bond." My hands loosen and I turn around slowly. There in the middle of the room is the tiny Jesus statue. Standing there almost completely rusted now.

"You remember me saying that the statue resembles your mental state? The rust Andrew. It's chipping away. Your conscious mind is chipping. The pipes, filled with thoughts are cracking. The transportation for emotion is becoming unstable. Let it flow Andrew release your hate. Strike it down."

All the hate, all the fear, all the stress, all of it welled up inside me and I snapped. I charged at it with a fist held high. My hand came down on the statue hard, knocking it over and blooding my hand. I raised another and another, pummeling it. Blow after blow my hands became more covered in blood and rust. My thoughts began to blur with all the pain I've ever been put through. The statue just laid there on the ground, taking my onslaught of flying fists and flurried emotions. Eventually, my hands slowed and my emotions drained. I let my hand fall to my sides and I rest there in the middle of my bedroom floor on my knees. I felt...relieved. For once in a long while, I felt at peace. True peace. Not some false instated peace. Real tranquility. I closed my eyes and let my body rest.

"Done now?" A voice echoed in the stillness of the air. Elijah was still on speaker. My eyes shot open. I mumbled something to myself the resembled "No".

"Ok then. Your body is now forfeit. Nothing stands in my way of controlling you know. No more clouded thoughts or powerful rage is harboring me. Your mind is at its weakest...I am at my strongest..." Shit... My body begins to freeze up. New emotions come to my head. Thoughts. Words of foreign languages and a feeling of absolute terror. A feeling of fear for my own life.

"That's good now rise." My body stands, not on its own. I raise myself to a standing height and bloodied arms outstretched. The silver man, covered in blood arises from the floor and straightens himself upright. I turn slowly and back up to him. From what I can judge he is about a foot behind me. All my memories now flood my head, perhaps a last blessing from the devilish prophet.

All the happy days with Lilly...No more...All the better days of Janice's presence...Flooding from me...Every happy moment, every wonderful friend I've made, every pleasure of mortal life as I know them...No more. Something fades now into my head...noise...It wasn't till now I noticed I couldn't hear any sound at all. The noise of voices and forceful slamming carried its way into my room. I could see shadows moving underneath my door as well as my door being slowly broken down. The door bent and cried with every crush of the object on the other side. Over the commotion, I heard a rough man's voice.

"Hey! Stop her! I told you to keep her back! Someone grab her!"

"Let go of me! I need to see him! He'll open up for me, I promise! Dad! Open the door! Please! They're taking me away! Hey, let go of me! Help! Dad!" It was Lilly! She was trying to save me! She must have been trying for days now and only recently called the police. Her voice was soothing and comforting despite being spoken as a yell and worried. A tear found its way onto my face. The mark in the middle of my face began to burn a vengeance. It hurt, so did my hands, but nothing hurts more than watching your life come to a halt before your very eyes.

"Touching but we don't have to waste this day. Goodbye, Andrew." Elijah said than began to chant in some language I couldn't quite understand. My legs began to fold and my back started to arch. My body was starting to bridge with my legs going down and the rest of me beginning to level out. Something hit me at that time. I was poised in such a way I would descend on the statue.

My whole form hurt. My body wasn't meant to arch like this. As I was nearing the floor, the head of Jesus touched the base of my neck from behind. I wanted to scream or tell Lilly I loved her but my voice was shot. I couldn't even manage a squeak of fright. I Started to feel my bones crack and the Jesus head now starting to pierce my neck. Pain shot throughout my whole body and my mind began to shatter. All the mental insanity and physical pain began to make my body numb and my vision blurry. Pain sensors and nerves shut off and I could feel my body slip into darkness. Just as my vision was about to go completely black, I saw the head of the savior remerge out of the front of my throat, blood following and flowing behind it. I blinked one last time and took one last choking breath just as the door was broken down and people rushed in. The sharp, icy hands of death grabbed onto me and I fell from my once happy and vivid life into a foreboding and ever dark abyss, never to think or feel a thing again.

Chapter 7: Silver Is But An Heirloom

"I simply cannot believe that sorry fuck went and offed himself. How selfish!" I thought to myself as I drove in my SUV to go get Lilly. She must have been traumatized by this whole thing. There's no way in hell he ever deserved her. I just hope she'll be ok.

I pulled in the Crystal Heights Apartments to be met with a swarm of flashing lights, brightly colored vehicles and crowds of people. It was hard to maneuver through it all but I eventually came to a stop just outside the barrier set up by the crew. Lilly was sitting on the back of an ambulance with her makeup streaming down her face. She looked a wreck. Son of a bitch, she was hurt by this. I honked my horn and she looked up quickly and saw my car. She gave a brief thank you to the paramedic and ran over to my vehicle. She hopped in and slammed the door and started going on about how awful the whole thing was and that she was so scared and that there was nothing she could do. I hushed her with a hand on her head.

"Lilly, it's ok. You're save now. I know, I know, there there. Let's get going shall we?" She sniffled a little and nodded her head slowly.

"I'll call movers later to come by and get your things. For now, let's just get home and get some well needed rest." She nodded again and rested her head on the window, the whole ordeal still fluttering in her head.

I put the car into reverse and backed cautiously out of the scene. I spun the wheel back and shifted to drive. I made my way out of the crowd and was just about get out of the complex when something made me slam on the brakes. Lilly braced herself on the dash while I crushed my foot into the brake, a look a frustration and shock on my face. An old man had ran in front of us, waving his arms wildly. We came to a rest, slightly cocked sideways on the road. He ran over to the window and I gladly rolled it down, ready to give this guy hell.

"So sorry miss! Please hear me though!"

"What the hell do you want you old fuck! You almost got ran over! Would could possibly that important!?" My pretty face twisted into anger.

"Sorry! But I had to stop you! You see, a neighbor asked me to give you these. They had begun to take things from the home and he wanted me to stop you to tell you. I managed to grab some of it before all of it was removed from the premises."

He went back to his car for a moment before returning and offering a box to me. At this time, I'm more than skeptical. I gave a look at Lilly who was in desperate need of rest. The faster I could get out of here, the better. I turned back to him and reached out the window. I took the box of things. It was rather heavy. Putting it all in the back seat, I gave a quick glance in. Some papers, clothes, personal things and souvenirs, and a faded CD case. I rustled it free and scanned over it. Most of the words were etched out. I flipped it over to find a set of numbers scratched into it. 5163742. What did that all mean? No fucking idea. Looked like it at seven tracks to its name. Before I could make out the words, the old man made his presence known again.

"So yea, his things are being taken into the police station to be looked at for evidence, given the circumstances of the death." I scoff to myself at his words. Well I should probably thank him. He did kind of go out of his way for us.

"Thank you so much for this. Um. I really must get going though. So I'll let you go. Again, thank you so much. I'm Janice, his ex-wife."

"No problem Janice. My name is Elijah. Elijah Wilkes." He extended his hand meaning for a handshake. I'm not one for handshakes but it was only polite. I grabbed his hand with my right hand and gave a quick shake or two before drawing back into my SUV.

"Take care now!" With that he turned and went on the other side of my car. He hopped in his ramshackle rusty old truck. His engine roared to life and moments later, was off in the direction of the scene once again. I clicked my shifter to drive and made my way to the exit of the apartments. Maybe now that I have Lilly, things will be back to normal. She was fast asleep as of now, tired from all the stress and mental torment. I made a left out of the apartments and was quickly on my way home. Maybe when I get there, I'll pop in that CD just to see what kind of music this fucked up guy listened to. The title seemed nice enough at least. Carved in Stone by Messiah of Silver.

Floyd Pinkerton

Lee Sherman. Alias Floyd Pinkerton (and variants thereof). Twentysomething starving artist. Works as English T.A. Lives in Iowa near the site of a famous archeological hoax.

An Image in the Light

By: Floyd Pinkerton

When I see lightning, it dissolves my knowledge and reason, allowing primal fears to spill into my mind. It was 11:38 when the clock went out. The lights were already off, and I was in bed trying to force myself out of consciousness.

I was long past the phase where I half-believed closing my eyes, facing the opposite direction from the window, and drawing the covers over my head would help facilitate sleep, and was helplessly moving my vision around to whatever wasn't pitch black, waiting to feel tired enough that I would ignore my irrational anxiety. But it was all too much for my mind. The ghostly howling wind, the rain beating down mercilessly on my house and lawn, the thunder like the sky being torn in a monstrous cacophony, and, most of all, the vicious flashes which came seconds or less before the thunder and painted my backyard with eerie light that made it look like a cartoon.

I was aroused from the sort of hypnosis the storm had thrown upon me by a different sort of lightning. On my walls it looked like irregular flashes from a camera just outside my window, and there was no sound of thunder to accompany it. The normal lightning seemed to have been turned off to make way for this. I looked out the window to see what was casting the light on my bedroom wall.

To my surprise, it wasn't coming from above the treetops or behind the tall fence, but, apparently, from the middle my backyard, about twenty feet in front of the shed. I was transfixed. It was as if lightning from the four corners of the sky was converging in a spindle-shaped globule of light.

No, they weren't converging to form it. They were emanating from it.

The conglomeration of light sparked on and off in an irregular strobing effect, maintaining perfect silence. It was an otherworldly pink, like some sort of neon rose. After one of the times it winked out, it was dark for so long I thought the terrifying display was over. But after seven seconds or so it came back for two heartbeat-like flickers, and I could discern inside the blinding oval, as clear as the words on this page, the silhouette of a human figure.

After that, the light was gone. The regular lightning returned like a faded-in scene in a film, and its angry illuminations proved there was nothing and no one in my backyard.

My mind searched for an explanation for what I had just seen. It's still searching.

When I see lightning, it always brings me back to that night. My life-long fear is still there, but now there's a long-standing mystery on top of it. With each bright gash that cuts through the dark sky, I almost expect to learn the answer.

I'm afraid that one day I really will.

Izzy's Ghost Story

By: Floyd Pinkerton

Fossberg is a joker. That's the first thing you have to understand, and that's what I want to make clear before you read my account of the occurrence. I'm sure he'll go to his grave chuckling over jokes no one ever got but him. He's sick that way. I'll find out years after the fact that things he told me were utter bull, and he thinks it's so damn funny that I never realized he was kidding.

I first met him at one of Chuck's parties. I asked him what he did for a living, and he said he was a doctor. Of course that much is true. When I asked him what kind he said he was an animal psychiatrist. Then he said to me with a straight face, "I work with collies who are borderline." Eventually I got it, and thought it was hilarious. It set the tone for our friendship. Anything serious he's ever said to me might only be a joke I haven't gotten yet.

So don't believe anything he tells you about "Izzy's Ghost Story." I can tell you the true whole story. You need look no further than this message, because there's nothing for him to supplement. His slant on the whole thing is probably much more entertaining than what I've typed out here. I'm not going to deny that. But if you want your book to be about the facts of actual hauntings, you should ignore it. He's not a reliable witness. He's a joker.

This is my story. I don't have any interesting tales of self-realization or coming of age like most people I know. I'm still a spinster at 29, and have no wonderful love stories to tell. I never got in a fight with Ron Howard at the Ames straw poll or got dug out of a snow bank by my trusty dog. No, this is my only story. I tell it well, and I tell it accurately.

For reasons that should be obvious by now, I didn't believe Fossberg when he said he'd seen ghosts in the house before. I was on a stretch of country road somewhere between Waukon and Decorah. It was pretty long odds that he'd been in the same abandoned house my car stalled next to, even if it was famous in local folklore.

I thought he was just playing off the spookiness of the situation. It was after dark, my car was dead, there was no sign of the solid obstacle I thought I'd hit, and the keys got locked inside when I was just sure the door wasn't locked. So I was already slightly freaked out when he started telling me creepy stuff to try to ramp up my fear even further. I think I did believe him for a moment, or at least I kept an open mind. But his description of being inside the house was what did it. I burst out laughing when I heard him say the ghosts were dancing flamingos. The signal was wavering, but he said he was coming to get me before we got cut off completely. He was a good hour, maybe hour and a half away from this place, and that was in good driving conditions. So I had a lot of time to kill.

I didn't want to wait in the rain, so walked up the gazillion steps up the hillside to take shelter in the house. I think Fossberg made me less scared of the house than I was to begin with, since the nonsense about it being haunted by flamingos just lightened my whole tone of thinking.

It wasn't that creepy a house either. It looked pretty modern. Of course it was run-down, but it wasn't bad enough that I thought the floor would collapse under me or the storm would bring the walls down or anything like that. I was in a big open room, like a living room that seamlessly turned into a kitchen toward one end, and I assume was a dining room somewhere in between. There were a total of five windows in various states of brokenness, and I could see a staircase and the entrance to a hallway. I was standing on a polished hardwood floor that had taken a beating. I still had a flashlight with me, which I'd been using to try to locate whatever it was I'd hit, so I wasn't in total darkness. It really wasn't that bad.

Things started to get to me pretty quick, though. There were odd creaking sounds. Nothing too unusual, but they set my nerves off every time. I kept thinking I saw something moving out of the corner of my eye. I was trying to look around this old house to pass the time, and all I was doing was jolting back and forth at every noise and shadow. Moving away from the walls and windows and door helped, because I couldn't worry that something was about to fall on me or jump out and ambush me. I decided to wait in the center of the giant room, where nothing could harm or scare me. Of course that didn't work out too well. I wouldn't be writing this if it did. Since you're reading this, you know it's gonna get scary. So I'll cut to the chase.

A bell sounded in the distance, and it struck me like a syringe to the spine. Now this wasn't necessarily paranormal. I've never been anywhere where a church or anything else rang a bell at midnight, but it's certainly conceivable. Still, it terrified me to hear it, so loud and clear and ominous.

As the sound faded away and I was trying to let my anxiety do the same, I heard something else. It was hard to make out from the rain and wind, but it sounded like whispering. I strained my ears to make it out. I walked around to try to find its source, but I was still too scared to go close to the walls. The sounds were coming from more than one place anyway. At least it sounded like they were.

I know things like that can be funny. One night at home I almost went nuts trying to find which room a tinkling sound was coming from. I followed the sound, but every time I went into the room it seemed like it must have been coming from I'd hear it coming from somewhere else. It turned out it was my neighbor's wind chimes, like 60 or 80 feet from the northwest corner of my house.

That was a real detour, but my point is I know acoustics are a strange thing. But it really did sound like there were weird little noises coming from all around, and that started right as the bell died away. The more I listened, the more it sounded like people were whispering. It sounded like just nonsense syllables at first. Sibilance and nothing else. But then I heard "Isabel." Then I couldn't hear anything but "Isabel." These horrible voices from every direction were calling my name.

I tried to talk to them. I felt crazy doing it, but it was all I could think of to do. I asked who they were and what they wanted. They just kept whispering "Isabel" over and over and over until the hail started.

The hail beating on the house either silenced the voices or just masked them. I kept sitting in the middle of the room, afraid to go anywhere else. I didn't want to be in this house, of course, but I didn't want to stand out in the storm either. It was around this time I noticed a rhythmic thumping noise. It was just one notch above being inaudible in the din of the hail. Just like the whispers were one notch above being drowned out by the sound of the rain. I felt like the ghosts were trying to make sure I heard them even as they were losing out to the storm outside.

I tried to find something to look at to take my mind off all this. The house was totally empty. No furniture, wall hangings, nothing. A couple light fixtures here and there, and screws and things that things used to be mounted on, but basically nothing to look at. The walls were painted white, and the blue pattern stenciled at the top were the only decorations or features of any kind.

This pattern was a bunch of vague, sort of flowery and clover shapes that ran along the wall just before it met the ceiling, and formed pairs of half-arches over the front doorway and the entrance to the hall. I watched them, trying to understand the pattern. I couldn't tell you how it went now, but when I was in that empty room all alone I analyzed that stenciling to within an inch of its life. It had two main segments that alternated, but were thrown off every so often by a third segment that looked like a bunch of confused butterflies. I figured it went ABABCABABC, but after a while that didn't work either.

I was pondering this when I thought I saw the pattern move. I should mention that the whole thing was askew. You could really tell that at the corners. So I thought that when I followed it with my flashlight like I was doing my brain tried to correct those imperfections. Like it was all an optical illusion. But things kept twitching and adjusting themselves. First it all happened in one place two segments out from a corner, but then all over the place. Then I saw one segment of the pattern crawl like an inchworm and replace another. I felt my whole body shudder and twitch involuntarily at the sight. I couldn't keep looking. I had to get my mind on something else.

Like the noises. There was still that thumping noise, and my ignoring of it failed as soon as I was ignoring the stenciling. The thumps came about once a second, and seemed to be grouped into fours. I don't think I noticed that right away, because it was faint at first, but it definitely had a sort of pattern to it. I connected them with the shadows moving in the hall.

You see, there was this light coming from what I assumed was a window at the end of the hallway. There was faint light coming in each of the windows. But I hadn't looked into the hallway. I was now sitting in the middle of the big room in total terror. I could just see the dim light coming out of the hallway, and there were shadows moving in it. They could've been trees or climber roses or something outside, but they looked less mundane the more I saw them move around. I shined a light at the entrance to the hall, but saw no movement, and of course that made the light from the window invisible. I called out and got no answer. I turned the flashlight off completely to let my eyes adjust. It began to look like people were pacing up and down the hallway, just out of my sight. I was scared, but I was more curious than scared. You'll find that's a recurring motif in this story.

But this time my curiosity didn't lead me to anything awful. I got up, walked over to where I could see straight down the hallway, and there was nothing. The noises continued, but they weren't being made my marching ghosts in that hall. I was never clear on what was casting the shadows, but that didn't bother me for long.

After I'd sat back down in my safe place in the open, I saw another thing moving. I was seeing lots of things like that out of the corner of my eye. It was my whole night, pretty much. But this was a more distinct sort of something, and it was coming right at me. I scrambled off the floor. I heard my scream echo through the big empty house, joined by the sharp thud of something striking the wooden floor. A series of smaller thuds followed as it hit the edges of boards while sliding across the floor.

It was a rock. Somebody had thrown a rock right at me from outside a window. I shined my light in each of the windows, but saw nothing. I was too afraid to walk up and look outside. Afraid somebody or something would pop up and scare me. I wasn't even sure which window the stone had come from, since when I traced its direction backwards it led to a blank wall. I wondered if it even came from outside. It wasn't wet.

I left my spot for good, because I didn't feel safe there anymore. I decided to see what other rooms there were. I walked down the hallway that sometimes had shadows. There were a couple bedrooms and I suppose a bathroom, but I didn't get to investigate them. I got hit by another rock.

By the time I realized what had happened, two more had pelted me. It was a shower of stones from above. I shined my light up at the hole I assumed they were falling through, only to see a solid ceiling. Besides some moss or mold or something it was totally intact. But these little grey-white stones were coming down on me, not hindered by the fact that they had no place to come from. They just kind of appeared at or just below the ceiling, popping up out of nothing. It was like watching popcorn pop. One hit my flashlight and it went off.

As you can imagine, I only stayed in the hallway a couple seconds. The rocks weren't falling in the big room, so I scampered back over there and watched the downpour while my breathing and heartbeat gradually slowed to normal operating pace. The flashlight was still semi-useful. I would hit it and it would go on for a moment at a time before dying again. It was enough to see what was going on.

Here's another odd thing: The stones weren't falling very fast. If they'd been dropped out of the ceiling under normal circumstances they'd come down and hit the floor in a second. A fraction of a second even. And it looked more like they were falling through the ceiling thanks to some kind of crazy Star Trek physics, so they were starting out much higher and should be falling even faster. That makes sense, right? They should've looked like streaks to me until they bounced off the floor and settled down. But instead I could see each individual stone falling in slow motion in the light of the inconstant flashlight. I'm sure it wasn't just a trick of the light.

This still didn't account for the rhythm I'd been hearing. It was starting to really bother me that I didn't know what was making it. I figured I'd covered this floor, so I walked up the staircase to investigate the next. I proceeded slowly, using the blinking flashlight to see if the steps ahead of me were broken or sloping. Sure enough, the rhythm got louder. At one point I thought I'd have to stop because the flashlight would just not work, but then it came back on.

I was on the second floor (which I think was the top floor) when my light died completely and utterly. I'd been banging it harder and harder without results, and finally threw it against the floor in frustration. I heard rolling batteries and realized I no longer had the option of trying it again. But before it went out I got an idea of the layout of the second floor. With the way the house was cut up, most of the floor was closed off in a single room. With the flashlight out, I saw there was a light coming from under that door.

This should have been impossible since the house didn't seem like it should have electricity and every fixture I'd run across had had the light bulbs taken out. What's more, there were moving shafts of dark in that light. The thumping was very loud now. There was something in that room. I froze at the thought of what that something could be.

Losing my light had taken its toll on my spirit, and the episode with the stones had convinced me that something had it in for me. The situation was more chilling than ever, and I imagined it would only get worse if I went into that last room. I was thinking about leaving the house and waiting outside despite the foul weather. As terrified as I was of the house, I was also afraid of living the rest of my life without ever knowing what was making that noise. As you can guess if you've read this far, curiosity won.

I forced my hand to turn the knob. I could have opened the door slowly, peeking through the crack, but I didn't. Not wanting to prolong this anxious uncertainty, I threw it open. It opened into a big dusty rectangular room illuminated by a sourceless light, completely empty except for five ghostly birds.

They looked like Thanksgiving turkeys straight out of the fridge. They had no heads, but their size, shape, and hints of pink told me they were flamingos. They looked solid and ethereal at the same time. They glowed, and I could partly see through them, but I could also see the textured flesh of a preserved dead animal. They danced in perfect unison to music no mortal ear could hear. Their featherless wings and long, goosebump covered necks beat and twisted to the same rhythm as their scaly feet. They hardly seemed to touch that unpolished wooden floor. Gravity wasn't doing its job right. But they were coming down with enough weight that the floor shuddered under them, and the steps to their dance could be heard far and wide.

I stared in awe for a while. It could have been a couple seconds or a quarter of an hour for all I know. Thinking back, it was strange how little I reacted. I didn't scream or gasp or shudder or fall down as my knees weakened. I just stood there transfixed.

The flamingos didn't react to me either. The dancing didn't screech to a halt. Nothing rushed at me or lunged at me or glared at me or shouted at me to get out. No phantom band materialized. None of the missing heads ever showed themselves. Nothing happened at all besides what was already going on when I opened the door. It continued on and on like a screen saver.

I don't know what it was that finally jarred me into action, but once I was going I didn't look back. I slammed the door and tried to run downstairs despite not being able to see the stairs. I overshot the whole staircase and sailed over the railing. I found myself back on the ground floor. I would find out later that I'd bruised myself badly and pulled the hell out of a muscle in my left arm when I caught my fall, but I didn't notice any of that at the time. There was nothing in my mind except the flamingos and the haven from them that existed outside the house. So I pretty much hit the floor running and didn't stop until I'd made it to my car. The rain and hail hardly slowed my pace. I couldn't see anything past a couple yards, but I still ran, falling and picking myself up a few times until I stumbled upon the road and traced my way to the car.

Then I waited there getting more chilled than I thought a living body could. I thought hypothermia would shut me down, but I could still feel my heart beating frantically. I don't think it had slowed down one bit when I saw lights coming toward me. Of course I was expecting it to be a ghost as much as a car, but it turned out to be the second option. I was so happy to see the freckly weasel face of Mark Fossberg illuminated by the dashboard light.

I climbed in and immediately started babbling about what I'd just been through. I tried to see if that supernatural light was still glowing in the house, but couldn't find anything behind the sheets of dark rain. So there was nothing to point out. But I told Fossberg about it and everything else. He didn't say a word until I came to the part about the flamingos.

"Knock it off," he said. That threw me for a loop because I didn't know he was doubtful at all. I guess I can't read him.

"You don't believe that house is haunted?" I asked.

"Oh, I believe that much. I know it for a fact."

"Then why don't you believe I saw the ghosts too?"

"I saw real ghosts," he said with an anger I'm sure was feigned, "ghosts of people." After a pause, he added, "Those ghosts were dancing the flamenco."

I'm sure I yelled something at that point, but I'm not sure what.

Fossberg continued. "I told you about the ghosts and the flamenco dancing. You misheard that and so you made up a story with the wrong kind of ghosts. Everything else in your story is taken from other haunted house accounts, too." He started listing what he thought were clichés until I yelled at him some more.

"You must have seen dancing flamingos! Those are the ghosts in the house! I saw them!"

"Just shut up," he said. "I don't believe your ghosts exist."

We said nothing for the rest of the car ride.

Since then it's come up a few times between us. He mocks me over it. He tells people about "Izzy's Ghost Story" in an insulting way. Lots of folks think it's funny, but I can tell that he can tell that it's true.

I just know he said "flamingos," and I sure as hell know what I saw. You can put that in your book, and I hope you throw out whatever Fossberg told you. I'm sure he could give you a fascinating prequel to my experience in the haunted house if he'd tell it to you straight, but he won't. He's too much of a joker.

"P" Is for "Phobia"

By: Floyd Pinkerton

I don't want to make it sound like I have a wicked stepmother. She's hardly a bitter old witch. She was a college student when my dad first brought her home to meet me, and was full of youthful spirit. She wasn't much different from the teenage babysitters I'd had, except for the part where she moved in permanently. She was beautiful in a modest way, with brown hair she wore in a conservative hairstyle and a fondness for turtleneck sweaters in muted colors. Overall, she had and still has all the qualities of a first-rate *Nick-at-Nite*-worthy mother. The worst thing she ever did was make me surrender to a monster.

Since before I can remember, there was a vicious fiend in our house. I heard it gurgling and splashing and roaring and hissing and groaning. I saw it slither and twitch and glisten in the dim light. It would taunt me by appearing around corners then quickly retreating to its den. I never saw its teeth, but its surrogate jaws seemed powerful enough. It nested right around the corner from my bed. And the worst part was, every adult wanted me to feed it. I would have rather let its meals go to waste in my training pants.

There's only one viable floor in our house. My dad stopped being Mr. Fix-It when my first mom left. Now he's got a different career and different hobbies. He probably doesn't even believe himself when he says he'll finish the house one day. As a result, the attic is a woolly death trap of fiberglass insulation, and the basement is a leaky dungeon. We basically have a house with one floor, and naturally there's only one bathroom. I've never really believed in my heart of hearts that that room was safe. Sure, the old house is full of places where creatures could hide in and move through unseen. I recall a tall and cadaverous headhunter in the basement, and a sheet-like jellyfish that slipped through the walls to visit every closet and cupboard. But the one in the plumbing scared me the most. I continued to fixate on it long after the other monsters had disappeared.

My only episodic memory of my natural mother was her keeping me safe from this monster. It comes from the period of my life where memories are as hazy as dreams, and it's hard to tell which I'm recalling. But as I see it in my mind's eye, I was walking to the bathroom to take care of business like a big boy when I caught a glimpse of something horrifying in the twilight of the night light. A dark thing that gleamed like wet tar held the toilet lid just a tiny bit above the seat.

"Mommy, Mommy!" I cried. She came rushing in to see what was the matter, scaring the monster back into its hiding place. By that time the big boy ship had sailed, but my mom comforted me, changed me, and acted like she believed me. She even stayed in bed with me so I could go to sleep, even though I knew the monster sometimes ventured out of its watery lair.

But soon she was gone. My dad was understanding, but rather stern. After much coaxing, lecturing, and a few harsh words, he eventually convinced me that every other toilet in the word was safe, and even this one was safe during the daytime. I still believed in a plumbing monster that could harm me in the night, but this was the greatest victory he could hope for. I made the transition from training pants to Treasure Planet underwear and started kindergarten only one year later than a child without a disabling phobia would have.

There was still the problem of the night. It didn't matter if the lights were all on indoors, or if my big strong dad was right there to protect me. I just couldn't risk a monster attack. Even leaving my bed seemed like a putting my life on the line. So my dad let me keep an empty Smuckers jar next to my bed.

By the time the new mom moved in I had advanced to a Ball jar hidden in my nightstand that I was expected to wash with the dishes every evening. Little else had changed. By then I wasn't convinced that there was a monster, and I told my dad that I didn't really believe in it, but I was still scared. That sort of fear that makes you believe you'll fail a test you've already handed in just because you told your friends you'd nailed it. That strong fear without strong belief is in everyone, and it was certainly present in me all the nights I sat on the edge of my bed with my most sensitive organ resting on the lip of a cold glass jar. It was humiliating, but the humiliation never outweighed the fear. That is, until the first time my stepmother cleaned my room. I snuck the jar out and vowed to never use it again. I thought I could do better for my new mom, my new friend. This was a terrible mistake.

My dad's work kept him away from home more and more. Pretty soon my mom was caring for me almost exclusively. It was like I'd exchanged one parent for another, one of no real relation who would have been in her early teens when I was born. It felt different having her in charge, and very different having to answer to her when I did something wrong. Before long, I was doing something wrong pretty often.

It was because of the plumbing monster, of course. When night fell and the house was full of mysterious noises I couldn't bring myself to approach those porcelain jaws. I certainly tried. I would walk out of my bathroom and into the hallway, turn the corner, walk up to the open bathroom door, then realize I just couldn't do it.

My last trip to the bathroom at sunset had to last me until the morning light. Some nights, perhaps most, I made it. It was hard drifting off without feeling comfortable inside, and I'd wake up with a bladder so full it was excruciating, but I could manage it some nights. On many nights I didn't. I'd toss and turn and feel worse and worse. It would get to where it seemed like there was a sea urchin nesting in my pelvis, sticking its spines deeper and deeper into my soft tissue. Eventually I'd hear that familiar hissing sound, then fall asleep in the damp, muggy warmth.

No one even mentioned it the first time it happened. I knew my mom knew, because she had my bed looking and smelling fine when I came home from school, but she didn't say a word about it. She probably thought it was a fluke, and didn't want to embarrass me over something that would never be important again. But by a week or so, maybe a month, a clear trend had emerged.

My mom confronted me about the accidents. I let slip that I wasn't really a bed wetter because I was always awake when I peed. She went through the roof.

"You'd better have a good reason for that," she said in a very mom-ish tone.

"I do!" I asserted. "Somebody's keeping me out of the bathroom, and I can't always hold it 'til I fall asleep."

As I recall, that explanation calmed her down a little. It didn't last, though.

"Oh, sweetie," she began, "if you ever need to use the bathroom badly and I'm in there, or your father is, you can just knock on the door and tell us. It's not hard to hurry up and let you go. You don't have to wait if you can't."

"It's not you. It's the monster that lives in the plumbing." That set her off worse than before.

When my dad came home, I ran to him sobbing.

"Daddy, Daddy! Mommy's being mean to me!" were my most likely words.

Once we'd both presented our cases, all he had to say was, "Listen to your mother."

She said the sort of things I'd heard for years. Monsters weren't real. All the noises in the house had explanations, even if my father with a background in home repair couldn't explain every one. No adult had ever seen this monster. My parents used the toilet at night all the time, and they were both still alive. These arguments were old hat. I dismissed them all, and refused to promise I'd risk my life to protect some cloth.

My mom "forbid" me from wetting the bed, but that didn't mean anything. She shot down my dad's suggestion that I go back to using a container.

"We don't live in the nineteenth century," she told me in an unnecessarily educational outburst. "You do not get to keep a chamber pot under your bed. We have the modern miracle of indoor plumbing and you are going to use it, day or night. Do I make myself clear?"

Nothing was resolved that day. The only change to the status quo was that I got yelled at each time I lost control of my body during the night. But it wasn't long before my mom came upon a means of enforcing her ban on bedwetting.

It was a night like many others. I was lying in bed filled with fear and urine. Without the option to void my aching system, I was trying to fall asleep when I happened to cough. My mom was fortunate enough to be in earshot.

"Are you awake in there?" she called through the wall.

"Yes."

"Do you have to pee?"

I paused, not sure if it was worse to lie or to deal with the consequences of telling the truth. She spoke again before I answered.

"Just to be safe, you should go pee."

I got out of bed, turned on my light, and walked out my bedroom door sideways, with my back to the northern half of the doorframe. That way I could see and react if the monster lunged out of the bathroom. The room was in darkness, but I could see just enough to tell something was moving. I stood there for some time, trying to summon up the courage to walk forward and turn on the light.

"Are you in the bathroom yet?" my mom asked from the other room.

"Almost." I kept my feet planted well away from the bathroom door as I leaned forward and stretched my left arm out. It took a couple tries to hit the light switch, but when I succeeded my fears were confirmed.

The toilet lid was about halfway up. The monster especially bold that night. I could see it clearer than ever before. Its body was a very dark reddish orange, almost like molasses. A long strip of glistening flesh was lolling over the seat like a tongue. A nozzle-like appendage was sticking out sideways to its left. But the worst part was smack in the middle, and was holding the lid up. It was a long neck or tentacle that ended in a single eye. Its was smooth and bright orange, like fire trapped in a marble. It had a pupil shaped like four-armed starfish, which glared at me with unfathomable malice.

I was only half-surprised by this scene. My belief in the plumbing monster had been eroded over the years, but part of me had known it was real all along. Most boys in my place would have wet themselves then and there, but I was a veteran of monster encounters, and I didn't waste much time before I acted.

"Mommy, Mommy!" I shouted at the top of my lungs. "The monster's here! Come see it!" Once I heard her coming I ran back into my room and dove under the covers. I hoped to hear a scream as she saw the monster, but instead I heard a stern lecture.

"Young man, we have been over this. There is no monster in the plumbing. That's what little kids believe, not ten year olds."

I came out from under the covers to argue face to face. My mom was standing my bedroom doorway wearing a nightgown in some muted color.

"But I just saw it! It had a tongue and a big orange..."

"People get put in the crazy house for saying things like that. Now stop telling me nonsense, stop making a racket, and go finish what you got up to do."

I protested, but she marched over to my bed, grabbed me by the wrist, yanked me out of bed, and led me around the corner. She opened the toilet lid and pointed at the bowl, which contained nothing but clear water. She only said one word: "Go."

"It'll just come back," I explained, but my mom was resolute.

"I'm right here. Nothing's gonna happen to you." Then she turned to face the wall and give her boy a little privacy.

I hoped this grown-up was enough to keep the monster at bay, but I doubted it. I reached to lift up the seat, and jumped back when I saw something dart out of the hole at the bottom of the bowl. Seat and lid both fell down with a clatter. A "tongue" stuck out between them and licked its "lips."

"It's back!" I yelped as I grabbed for the doorknob. My mom stopped me.

"There's nothing here," she said, which was true at the moment and probably true by the time she had looked. She moved to block the door, faced me, and repeated the command. "Go."

I began another argument, but she cut me off.

"I don't want to hear another word out of you, young man. Just go."

I remember staring into my reflection in the toilet lid as I procrastinated over lifting it. When I finally did, there was nothing menacing underneath. I lifted the seat up. Still nothing. I paused. I opened the hole in the front of my tighty whities, then paused some more. I guess I stalled for too long.

Without warning, my mom took hold of my penis and aimed it at the toilet bowl.

"Pee," she ordered.

"But there's a monster!"

She stung my eyes with a look that injected terror into my blood, then stared expectantly at my prepubescent private parts. "If I have to wash your sheets one more time, you'll be better off with the monster," she spat.

As if it heard its name called, the monster began to make a racket. I heard a loud and lusty "glug glug glug!" Large bubbles rose to the surface. I closed my eyes, afraid the creature would show its awful face again. The water that had been welling up in them streamed down my face. I tried to jerk myself away from my mom, but it was no use.

"Pee!" she shouted, her fingernails digging into my skin.

"The monster's right here!"

"I don't care if it is!" she countered venomously.

What choice did I have? I somehow blocked the fear and shyness out of my brain and concentrated only on the muscles in my body. There was a drizzle for a few seconds before my equipment seized up.

"Keep peeing!" my mom barked, as if I had stopped on purpose. I summoned another tentative trickle, which relieved pressure from my aching bladder in fits and starts before finally gaining strength and becoming a useful stream. I felt like I stood there for hours in the spotlight with the lurking monster and the furious stepmother who didn't trust me with my own penis. My face was wet with tears, and my chest and throat were periodically seized with hiccough-like weeping. The outpouring from my urinary tract finally ebbed, then stopped entirely.

"Are you done?" my mom asked. All I could do was nod. She shook my penis like a dog trying to snap a snake's neck, freeing me of the final droplets. Then she tucked it back into my underpants and flushed the toilet. I just stood there, head hanging low.

"That wasn't so bad, now, was it?" she said. Then she shooed me out of the room because she needed to sit on the toilet she'd proven harmless.

I didn't let the plumbing monster keep me out of the bathroom after that. I was more worried about the monster who slept with my dad. Over time, even those harsh feelings faded away. I was a child with an overactive imagination, and she'd solved that problem without even having to pay a psychiatrist. Before too long, I'd forgiven her and forgotten the monster. It was all buried in the past.

On a night not so long ago, something exhumed that old memory and phobia.

My dad started renovating the bathroom before he had to leave town, and now a large rectangle has been skinned from the western wall. I expect it to be there for some time, and I've made the most of it. It's actually pretty interesting.

If you look in the right direction you can see yards of open space in the wall, with nails jutting out like teeth. There are gaps in the boards leading to more empty space that's impossible to see. There are spiderwebs everywhere in there, so I know that there are not only many spiders living in our walls but a population of insects to sustain them. There are also scraps of paper, chips of red terra cotta from a potentially beautiful brick wall buried somewhere out of sight, rocklike fragments of other building materials, and other less obvious things. I fished one out using a coat hanger because I was so curious. I thought it was probably a rotten old banana peel, but I wondered how it could have fallen inside the wall. It was actually a dead bat.

There's a whole country in the walls that I never see. That was an intriguing and somewhat disquieting realization. So the whole idea of hidden creatures was fresh in my mind the night of the event I'm about to describe.

It was the middle of the night, I was in bed, and something seemed wrong. First it was a strange noise, then the vague impression of something moving in the dark.

My mild unease escalated to anxiety when I heard what I could have sworn was the laptop on my desk closing. My heart raced, and I curled into a fetal position, unsure what else to do. I hadn't been this frightened by nothing in years.

It was childish. There is nothing in the dark that isn't there when the lights are on. The rational part of me had fully realized that years ago. But the irrational, emotional part still responded like a little boy to the slight suggestion that there was some Bogeyman in my room. I felt a very strong sensation of wrongness that seemed to permeate my entire darkened room like some supernatural poison and filled my entire body with profound disquietude.

I also had to pee. Eventually I would have to get out of bed, monster or no monster. I really wished I wasn't in that situation. I wished I knew for certain that the sounds were just the house settling and the movement was only in my mind. I wished I could just forget my fears and go to sleep. I wished I could find relief of my need without getting out of bed and moving through a potentially demon-haunted room. But no amount of wishing could erase the fear in my mind or the urgent sensation in my bladder. I had to face the unknown terror to get to the bathroom.

This is silly, I told myself. I'm a teenager in high school afraid to go pee because there could be a monster in my room.

On further reflection, it was even sillier than that. Hundreds of times every year I thought I was seeing something or hearing something in my darkened room, and it had never once turned out to be anything. Not even a mouse. The only times I'd "seen" a "real" threat were years ago when my rational mind was rudimentary and I was almost a different person. When I thought about how unreasonable what I felt was, my hand barely hesitated in switching the lamp on.

"Don't be afraid," a voice from the direction of my desk said. My blood chilled, and the air in my room grew thin. Half illuminated by the lamp on my nightstand, sitting on my desk, was what I can only describe as a monster.

Its shadowy shape recoiled from the light. Then it straightened itself into a rippling sheet and poured down the side of my desk, collecting on the chair next to it. The wooden backing hid most of it from the light and my vision, so all I could see was a dark pile of something with little legs or feelers twitching about. My verbal reaction to this spectacle wasn't exactly profound.

"Oh...my...God. A monster."

"I suppose you could call me that," the thing said. "I'm not in any of the planet's major phyla."

"What do you want with me?" I asked it. I suppose I should call it "him."

"Nothing. I came here to take someone home. He died here years ago, but we couldn't retrieve the body until now."

I was awestruck. I don't think I need to explain the ramifications of what I'd just seen and heard, or the many avenues of speculation it opened up. It just changed everything I thought I knew.

"How did you get in here?" I asked.

I was expecting to hear something about magic, parallel universes, folded space, or other such wonders. His answer was, "Through the dryer vent, across the basement ceiling, through the heat register, and over the desk that's blocking it." That made sense, because that register was one of several that weren't connected to ducts and simply led to cavities in the basement's open ceiling. More of my dad's unfinished work. "I'm sorry to intrude on your bedroom, but I can't get to the body without going through here."

"Where is this body?"

"We're not sure, but we've narrowed it down. Getting it to its rightful resting place will be harder than finding it."

Throughout the conversation I thought about turning on the overhead light and getting my camera out of my desk. I never did, because I was afraid to leave my bed. The monster seemed friendly enough, but I thought he might turn nasty if he thought I was going to impede his mission or jeopardize his secrecy. There was also the fact that I'd woken up with an extremely pronounced and persistent erection that would have been obvious once the covers were out of the way. So I stayed in bed while my guest went about his task.

The bunched-up monster startled me when he began to move in strange ways. I guess he was looking around, but there wasn't any continuous motion, and the jerks and shudders weren't localized to any one part. His whole body would twitch and reposition itself every few seconds, as if I were watching video that was randomly fast-forwarded every so often.

I was startled even worse when he suddenly made a move for the window. I was interested in seeing what he looked like, but his speed and the low light were both working against me. He fell out of the chair and rapidly scuttled to where he was adhering to the window next to my bed. "Scuttled" might be the wrong word, since it reads like a sound effect and this was without any noticeable sounds, but it's the best way I can describe the lightning-quick movement of this thing that was almost all legs. When he was on the window he was behind the curtains, so I didn't see many details as he unlatched the window and forced it open. He accomplished the latter task by scrunching himself up like an inchworm then straightening out.

This might seem funny to read, but it was unnerving in person. Every one of this thing's movements made it seem scarier. Sometimes it's hard to write "him" instead of "it."

After opening the screen he scuttled backwards into the hallway, turned himself around in a quick fluid motion, and disappeared into the bathroom. I soon heard the distinct gravelly sound of something moving inside the wall. It's a sound I've gotten to know well, both from my dad's handiwork and from the mice and bats that have been in the walls over the years. At least, I thought they were all mice or bats.

Again I considered fetching the camera, but the monster was back before I knew it, giving me a little start. He was carrying a cigar-shaped bundle on his back. He paused in the middle of the floor, probably thinking about how he was going to carry this outside, and the final foot or so of his body was in the light. I was finally able to see something of this monster, but my attention was drawn to the thing poking out of the cloth wrapping.

It was a silvery grey head about the size and shape of a furless male raccoon's head. The mouth was sort of like a wildcat's, and there was a mosaic of scales where the nose should have been. Appendages growing from the sides of its lower jaw had broken off, forming stumps of various lengths. There were two pairs of gaping holes where I assumed the eyes had been. They must have been much smaller than I thought, just like so many other things I remembered from my childhood. It didn't look scary at all. It looked sad.

This monster, which probably had family and friends, had died far away from home, and sat rotting in our wall instead of being laid to rest properly. He had never meant me any harm, but I'd hated him. I got a little choked up.

"I'm sorry if any of us have frightened you," the live monster said to me before he moved along. "We bear no ill will toward the educated chordates. We wish you the best of everything."

I didn't know what to say.

I did finally find my tongue just before the monster disappeared into the night with his departed comrade.

"Nobody's going to believe me," I told him. He paused on the windowsill.

"I'll see what I can do about that." With those words he crawled out of the house, closing the window and screen behind him.

Once he was gone I walked into the bathroom and used the toilet without fear. I smiled as I transformed the water's calm surface into a foamy yellow tempest. This room would never be dangerous again. Better still, I understood that it had never been dangerous in the first place.

The next morning there was a card lying on my nightstand. It was a photograph of one of the monsters resting on a bed of rocks on a sunny seashore. I turned it over. The back read, "Hot Spot 11, C. J. R. Boygins, 30949-53." Below the English was a line of blocky hieroglyphics and another of tangled squiggles and circles. I now held in my hands the proof I had never had before.

My mom was in the bathroom, but I couldn't wait. I pounded on the door a few seconds after I heard the shower shut off.

"Mom, Mom! I've got something to show you! It's incredible! Are you decent?"

When she let me in, I held out the photograph. She adjusted the fuzzy white bath towel she was wearing and leaned over to get a close look, trying to focus her contact-free eyes. She didn't say anything. I stared at the photograph too as I told her about my monster encounter the night before.

Then I realized something that made me stop my story mid-sentence.

The monster in the photo was long and thin, and its body shone in the sunlight. That much matched how I pictured the plumbing monster. This monster was an orange-tan color, not far from human flesh. Besides the mammal or reptile-like head and the unfathomable shapes at the other end, its body was entirely covered in armor divided up into segments. Each segment had a pair of spindly legs like on a daddy longlegs, and many had a shorter secondary pair with fingers, suckers, or both. All in all, it matched the bits of the monsters I had glimpsed the night before, but bore almost no resemblance to the one I'd spent most of my life fearing.

The most troubling part was that it had four blue eyes with round black pupils. I hadn't seen a trace of that bathroom beast in years, so I couldn't be sure I remembered exactly what it looked like, but that diamond-pupilled eye from my memories haunted me. That part had to be accurate.

"This isn't the right monster," I mumbled quietly as my brain soaked up the disquieting implications. "This just proves that the house's monsters are real, and the plumbing one is still at large."

My mom smiled, looking genial and maybe a little condescending. "Oh, sweetie," she began, "I know for a fact there's no monster in the plumbing."

"How?" I asked with wavering voice.

"Because," she replied in a stern tone. For a moment I thought that was all she had to say, but she continued to explain her reasoning. "...It crawled out of there years ago."

I just stood there dumbfounded. Is this a joke? I wondered. Is there more to it? The silence was suddenly broken by a gurgling and churning noise. It was louder than any of the strange noises that normally permeated the house, and sounded even less like it belonged in a human dwelling. But it wasn't coming from the toilet, the tub, the sink, or any of the walls around me. It was emanating from the middle of my mom.

I should have looked away when she let the towel drop to the floor, but somehow I couldn't. I was paralyzed, eyes wide, as my nude stepmother turned around, bent over, and placed a hand on either side of her round bottom. With her fingers pressing into her flesh, turning the rosy post-shower hue into a deathly white, she pulled her cheeks outward. Her anus puckered, domed, and widened. I could see something that didn't belong. The orifice grew wider and wider, finally stopping at four inches in diameter. Much wider than that was the partly extruded sphere. In an instant, its molasses surface retracted to reveal the fiery orange eye from my traumatic childhood memories.

"It's in my plumbing now."

ABOUT THE AUTHOR

Andrew Movitz, known online simply as ClericofMadness, is an author and curator of internet horror stories. For more, please visit http://www.creepypasta.wikia.com.

The Creepypasta Wiki is a community-based literary initiative, which exists to collect, organize, and showcase weird, creepy, and horrific tales written by the denizens of the internet, for the denizens of the internet. ~~Not everything is safe for your eyes.~~ Nothing is safe for anyone. Turn back now.

9895472R00132

Printed in Great Britain
by Amazon.co.uk, Ltd.,
Marston Gate.